Gothic Blue Book III
The Graveyard Edition

Edited by
Cynthia (cina) Pelayo & Gerardo Pelayo

Copyright © 2013 Burial Day Books

All rights reserved.

ISBN-13: 978-1493587100
ISBN-10: 1493587102
Cover art by Abigail Larson www.abigaillarson.com

We dedicate this year's Gothic Blue Book to Richard Matheson, a genius writer who gifted us a horrific legend, a cursed house, a monster on the wing of an airplane, explorers who travelled the universe and so much more. Your literary work has shaped so many and for this we thank you. Rest in peace – Richard Matheson (February 20, 1926 – June 23, 2013).

"Full circle. A new terror born in death, a new superstition entering the unassailable fortress of forever. I am legend. –Richard Matheson, *I am Legend and Other Stories*.

GOTHIC BLUE BOOK

CONTENTS

Introduction		7
Meg Belviso	MUST LOVE CHILDREN AND CATS	8
Die Booth	THE GHOST BRIDE	15
Melissa J. Davies	EZABELL FROWNED	21
Lance Davis	THE VIEWING	28
Nicole DeGennaro	THE KEEPER	32
Mathias Jansson	DEAR MADAME INSANE	36
K. Trap Jones	THE BASEMENT	37
Michael Kellar	THAT WHICH REMAINS	45
Edward J. McFadden III	SINS OF OUR MOTHER	46
Jessica McHugh	AUNTIE GRAVE	54
Georgina Morales	A DIARY OF MADNESS	61
Cortney Philip	DIARY OF A DOORMOUSE	67
Jennifer A. Smith	AND ALL THE TRIMMINGS	71
K.R. Smith	THE BALLAD OF DRUNKEN JACK	74
Peter Adam Salomon	THE QUESTIONER'S APPRENTICE	77
Jay Wilburn	REST	85
About the contributors		92

INTRODUCTION

The measurements of about three-to-four inches in width and about seven inches in height, ranging from thirty-six to seventy-two pages in length seem the satisfactory enough space in which to house terrifying little tales.

Gothic Blue Books were descendants of chapbooks and peaked in popularity between the late 1800s and early 1900s. They were abridgements of Gothic novels, and they were very cheap garnering them the nicknames of "Shilling Shockers" or "Sixpenny Shockers." These miniature tales of dread and despair that took readers through darkened castles, cursed abbeys, and homes layered in sin, ghosts, demons and death were not well-received by literary critics. In fact, the general populous of the time frowned upon the consumption of such fiction. Still, these stories were loved by many, so much so that very few originals remain as they were made with inexpensive material and being read and reread so often withered the pages away. Our attempt at reviving this tradition is to bring the reader traditional, Gothic horror, with the delight found in those original Gothic Blue Books. Of course, our work comes with modern twists.

In this collection you will find many restless ghosts and many tortured minds. As in the traditional Gothic tale you will certainly find instances of severe revenge. We ask that you visit with each of our wonderful writers in these pages. They have painted a marvelous Gothic world for you to visit. We hope that you enjoy this, our third, Gothic Blue Book – The Graveyard Edition.

Cynthia (cina) Pelayo
Gravedigger/Publisher
Burial Day Books

MUST LOVE CHILDREN AND CATS
Meg Belviso

Todd Jakeman didn't like children, but he liked Whitney Bloom enough to overlook the fact that she had one. Whitney wanted to be careful, she said, about bringing strange men into her daughter's life so Todd got to enjoy several childfree months of dating before it became an issue. He knew it was coming. She'd started to drop hints about him meeting the girl. The kid's photo seemed to loom larger and larger over Wendy's cubicle each time he stopped by. It didn't help that the kid was so unappealing: dumpy, stringy-haired and gormless, if the picture was anything to go by.

When the day finally came, it was as tedious as Todd expected. Laurel Bloom was in the second grade and liked three things: her cat, her collection of multicolor ponies and palindromes—words or sentences that read the same way backwards and forwards. Todd wasn't sure which of Laurel's three passions he hated the most, but the palindromes took an early lead. "It's the same frontways as it is backways!" Laurel explained to him each and every time she presented him with a new one. "Stop pots! Stop pots! Get it? You say it!"

"That's great," said Todd. "Why don't you tell it to your ponies?"

Whitney watched fondly as the kid skipped out of the kitchen. Todd had hoped the cat would follow her. Instead it hopped up on the chair that Laurel had just vacated and stared at him much the way Laurel herself did. It gave him the creeps.

"I'm so glad you and Laurel get along so well," Whitney sighed. "She needs a man in her life. Her teachers have been concerned. She doesn't stand up for herself at school, you know. Lets the other kids walk all over her. She just wants friends so badly."

Todd didn't need to hear it. He could just imagine how a kid like Laurel went over at school. He didn't want to spend the first five minutes the two of them had been alone this weekend talking about it. Whitney was standing at the cutting board chopping something up for dinner, wearing those little shorts he liked. Maybe Laurel would leave them alone long enough to have some fun...

Just as Todd moved to get up the full, fat, hairy weight of Fuzz the cat landed in his lap. "Hey!"

"Fuzz," said Whitney. "That was very rude."

Fuzz settled himself more firmly on Todd's lap and plucked at his linen trousers with his claws.

"Dammit!" Todd whispered, trying to pry the tiny curved blades out of his pants. "That's Ralph Lauren."

"He usually doesn't like anyone," Whitney said, as if Todd should take the attack on his pants as a compliment.

"Great," said Todd. "Is it, uh, time to put him out or something?"

"Put him out?"

"For the night? Isn't that a thing people do with cats?"

"Oh. Oh no," said Whitney. She slid the pile of orange things she'd chopped into a bowl. "It's not good to let them wander, even if they're fixed. They hunt the birds, get into traffic. Cats get lost around here all the time. Usually in the cemetery. I don't know what draws them to the place, but it takes forever to get them out. Some people have even petitioned for a chain link fence. Of course, that won't keep cats out if they're determined."

Fuzz sunk a thick white claw into Todd's thigh."

"Quit it!" he said. "Wait, cemetery? What cemetery?"

"Right over there," said Whitney, nodding toward the window. All Todd could see was the backyard at twilight: crooked hammock strung between two trees, cheap lounge chair for sunbathing, Laurel's jungle gym. "Over the fence," she said. "Our yard's right on the border. You didn't see it on the way over because we came from the other way, but it's huge. It's got mausoleums and everything. Creepy as hell so naturally Fuzz loves it. Silly cat."

Fuzz chose that moment to jump back on the table, angling his rear end into Todd's face. Todd seized his chance to cross the kitchen and press himself against Whitney and her shorts.

"A but tuba!" said Laurel, making a triumphant return to the kitchen and onto Todd's nerves. "It's the same frontways as backways! A but tuba. Get it?"

Todd Jakeman was liking children less and less every minute.

The cat hung around while dinner was served. He even got his own chair, next to Laurel and across from Todd, at whom the animal stared relentlessly all through the meal. Twice Todd dropped hints about cat hair getting into the food, but that only inspired Laurel to make up more palindromes like "cat food do of tac" which didn't even make sense. After dinner Whitney agreed to play some excruciating board game involving apples and sirens, which meant Todd had to play too. Eventually he volunteered to take the garbage out just to get away from it all.

"You're so sweet!" Whitney said when he offered. Jesus.

The cat followed him into the kitchen, though by now even a dumb animal had to know Todd couldn't stand the sight of it. It hadn't stopped staring at him since dinner. It had somehow managed to cover his pants in hair. Three times he'd caught it picking at the leather of his briefcase. "Just fifteen more minutes," he whispered to it. "Then it's time for bed." Laurel had bragged that Fuzz always slept in her room. Todd intended to lock him in personally.

He hauled up the bag of garbage and swung open the back door. It took all of 30 seconds to dump it into the trashcan, but in those seconds the cat streaked outside, down the steps and into the yard.

"Cat! Fuzz! Get back here!"

It paused just for a moment to glare at him, a yellow-eyed, flat-faced ball of spiky grey hair and smug vengeance, before dashing up and over the fence.

"Dammit," said Todd.

Of course Whitney was waiting when he came back into the kitchen, telling him not to leave the door open because the cat might get out. "He got out, didn't he?" she said when she saw Todd's face. "Oh god, did he go over the fence?"

Of course he went over the fence.

"Well, there's no hope finding him tonight," she said. "I'll try to think of something to tell Lauren. First thing tomorrow we'll go hunting in the cemetery."

She said "we" but her tone of voice somehow managed to convey that it really ought to just be Todd hunting the cat down. Had she forgotten he was doing something nice when it happened? How was he supposed to know the cat was lying in wait for his chance to escape? Wasn't he supposed to be the kid's very best friend? Wasn't he longing to cuddle up in her bed surrounded by the rainbow colored ponies?

It wasn't Todd's fault, but that didn't matter to Whitney. He could tell that by the weary and injured look she gave him when she took the kid up to bed. He might as well drive home now, because he wasn't getting anything from her tonight. In fact, he might as well consider the whole relationship over, because it was never going to go back to the way things were before. The kid had ruined everything.

But was Todd Jakeman really going to admit defeat to a kid? Or even worse, a cat? Todd Jakeman who'd finished marathons in Honolulu and Miami? Todd Jakeman who got the largest bonus in his section for three quarters running? Todd Jakeman who'd recently succeeded in bench pressing 205 pounds? Todd Jakeman could take care of a cat.

"What are you doing?" asked Whitney when she came back downstairs and found Todd fiddling with the flashlight.

"I'm going to get the cat."

Whitney rolled her eyes. "I told you. We'll look for Fuzz tomorrow."

Todd zipped up the front of his sweater.

Whitney sighed. "Are you coming?"

"I'll be up in a minute."

Whitney went upstairs. Good. Let her imagine he was wasting his time. She'd just feel all the more foolish when he dumped the cat in her lap.

It was easier to climb over the backyard fence rather than search for the cemetery gate. Plus Fuzz had come this way, so he might still be nearby. Perhaps Todd would find him just on the other side waiting to be carried back to his food dish and scratching post. He hoped so as he pulled himself over the pointed wooden slats. It was colder out tonight than he'd thought it would be and he'd left his jacket in the house.

He dropped to the ground inside the cemetery. The place was huge. Todd felt like he'd landed on some alien planet made of grass and stone. Grass, stone and no cats that he could see. *Dammit.* He walked further in. Now that he was here doubt began to creep in. What if he couldn't find Fuzz in the dark? He could just picture the look on Whitney's face if he came back to the house empty-handed. It would look a lot like the face she got at work when Todd screwed up the color copier - again. He glanced back over the fence to the house. He could see the light from her bedroom window and Whitney moving back and forth across it. She was talking to someone, probably the kid. Maybe she was telling her how Todd lost the cat.

Todd turned back to the cemetery. There—over by a pair of low shrubs, a cat's tail flicked up and out and disappeared. "Gotcha."

Todd moved quietly and quickly. Even a cat wouldn't hear him coming. Too bad it wasn't the right cat. Close up in the moonlight the fur he'd mistaken for Fuzz's muddy grey was bright orange. The creature let out a hiss and shot away down the hill.

"Dammit." The longer he stayed, the bigger the graveyard seemed to get. With no better ideas, he followed the orange cat as long as he could—a couple of minutes at most. Then the moon disappeared behind a cloud and the cat dodged out of sight. Todd turned on the flashlight, sweeping it in front of him as he moved. The grass whipped against the cuffs of his pants and the wind shushed through the trees overhead—it felt like being in a crowd of people whispering about him on all sides. He walked faster, as if he could outrun those eerie voices, and nearly collided with a pale, weeping woman.

Not a real woman, he realized after dropping his flashlight in shock. Just one of those creepy statues people put on graves and outside mausoleums. This one was an angel holding hands with a child.

A child. That reminded Todd why he was in this godforsaken place to begin with. Pudgy little Laurel with her palindromes, her cat and her irritating presence. He didn't want to be a father. He never asked to be a father. He hated to give up on Whitney. It had taken weeks of campaigning to get her to go out with him. Why did she have to ruin it by bringing the kid into it? They were all happier when he could just pretend Laurel didn't exist. He threw an angry glance over his shoulder at the house but he could no longer see it.

Todd blinked in confusion. He couldn't have walked that far so quickly. He ought to still be able to see the light from the house, he was sure. The cemetery wasn't *that* big, was it?

There was a rustling ahead. A white cat streaked across the grass. Apparently Whitney wasn't kidding when she said all the cats came to the graveyard. How many of the things were in here with him?

Todd spun around as one slithered past his leg. The moon had returned, making all the gravestones and the statues glow like ghosts. The cats looked like ghosts as well. He saw one, then another streak across the grounds, all heading to the same place—one of the marble tombs that dotted the grounds. A mausoleum. This one was nestled in a gentle dip in the land, a small, circular building surrounded by columns with a crown on top. Todd had never understood why people wanted things like it. It was like a building, a house to live in after death. This one looked almost like a temple, yet the person buried there was probably some housewife or tax accountant—not exactly a goddess in need of worship.

What did the cats want with it? Rats, he supposed. Or nests of birds. Something tasty-smelling if you were a cat.

At least he knew where Fuzz had gone. He marched forward with purpose: grab the cat and get out of this place. Get back to Whitney's kitchen, which was bright and warm, and out of this endless cemetery that was dark and cold. The whispering—the wind, that is—hadn't stopped. In fact it seemed to get louder the closer he got to the mausoleum. Louder, closer, more intense, like the hissing of a thousand angry cats.

Todd ran the last yards down to the tomb. The door was cracked open—was that normal? Well, what did it matter? There was nothing to steal in a grave. He pushed his way in with one shoulder. Cats slithered out of the way as he slipped inside. Someone had hung torches on the walls. Actual torches. Tiny ones flickering with real flames and black smoke.

The tomb was filled with cats. They lined the walls, covered the floor, jumped on and off the stone coffin in the center, its cover shoved over at an angle, as if someone had broken in to steal the body.

God, was that what had drawn all these cats to the place? A decomposing corpse? He peered into the opening but saw only darkness.

Todd swept the flashlight around the building. Cat's eyes glowed neon green one by one as the beam swept by them. He'd thought the place looked like a temple from the outside. It looked like a temple on the inside too, with ceramic urns and carved faces in the walls. Cat-like faces. And statues—weren't tombs supposed to have statues of saints and angels? This one had lions and cheetahs: the grave of some crazy cat lady.

And the cats had come to her. Dozens of them. Todd shook his head; sneezed explosively. God knows how much dander he was inhaling. One of them wound itself between his ankles, purring. He kicked it away.

"Fuzz?" God forbid the beast could learn its name. He drew the flashlight beam around the room again, slowly this time, taking in one cat after another: long-hair and short, striped and tabby, the ones with the blotches. What were they called? Calico. Persian, Siamese, Fuzz.

He sat half-hidden by a tremendous black Persian that was 25 pounds if it was an ounce. "Fuzz, get over here."

Todd stepped only half-carefully over the animals on the floor, enjoying the frantic movement as they got out of his way. Fuzz hissed as Todd gathered him up, his furry body going slack and heavy as possible. In the far corner another cat meowed with what sounded like disapproval. That call was picked up by the other animals in the room until they were all mewing and yowling in that peculiar way cats have that sounded like a woman screaming.

"Quiet!" Todd shouted.

The cacophony ceased.

He gathered Fuzz more securely in his arms. He heard a scrape of stone against stone that made his teeth hurt, then a faint whisper, soft as silk but clear. Todd whirled around, clutching the cat, fumbling with the flashlight. He couldn't see the moon through the door anymore. Something was blocking the opening. A column perhaps, a statue standing between him and the exit. The door couldn't be closed. Who would be so stupid as to shut it behind him? Not Todd Jakeman.

There was the coffin in the center. That was still open. In fact the top stone almost seemed to have moved since he came in, but torchlight could play tricks that way in the dark. Todd took a careful step forward, dragging his foot along the floor. When it came in contact with a cat he nudged it gently. He suddenly didn't feel like making the animals scatter. Just let them be. Even so the creature hissed, showing sharp needle fangs.

Fuzz wrapped his paws around Todd's wrist and pressed his claws into his skin.

"Fuzz! Stop it!" Another cat jumped at Todd's knee, knocking him off balance. He dropped the flashlight and grabbed onto the corner of the coffin for balance. Fuzz hit the floor with a shriek and took off. "Fuzz! Fuzz, dammit! I don't…"

He trailed off, not liking the way the stone walls seemed to absorb his words. Who cared about the cat? Who cared about the kid? Or Whitney? Or women? Or any of it? What was he doing in this rotten grave in the dark? If Laurel liked her cat so much she could come get it herself. Todd took a step towards the door and froze.

"Whitney?"

Someone was in the tomb with him. He could see her shadow on the wall. "Who's there?"

He almost thought he heard the whisper of a name, but it might have been the cats. They seemed to see her too. They came leaping off their perches to land on the ground in soft thumps, pushing against his legs. When Todd tried to move forward, they pressed against him.

"Who's there? Who are you?"

The shadow on the wall was black and solid, no matter how the torches flickered. Todd looked down for his flashlight, but it was hidden under the writhing bodies of the cats.

"Hey!"

Sharp claws dug into his ankle and he kicked out, sending an animal sprawling. Another of the creatures sunk its teeth into his calf. Something leapt onto his shoulder, slashing at his ear. Todd fell to his knees, instinctively covering his head, eyes and face. A single cat was yowling again somewhere, making his bloody ear throb. Warm bodies and fur pressed close on all sides. They bit at his fingers when he reached out blindly for the flashlight.

He heard the sound of silk across the stone and footsteps coming closer. Human-like footsteps this time; not the muffled, dreadful touch of cat paws. Todd lifted his face to look at her as she hovered over him. He saw only two eyes glowing neon green in the dark before a frenzy of teeth and claws descended on him.

In her bedroom, Whitney heard what sounded like screams coming from the graveyard.

They would really have to do something about those cats.

THE GHOST BRIDE
Die Booth

The first time, Carol thought it was a dream. She'd woken early in the morning with the feeling of something angular pressing into her thigh through the bedspread. That time, she hadn't been able to bring herself to even turn her head. From the corner of her eye, she could see something next to the bed. She shut her eyes and willed herself to ignore it; she'd researched sleep paralysis and lucid dreams and science soothed her back to sleep.

The last time, Carol turned her head. Dave's regular breathing beside her, the bedrock tick of the clock, the scratch of the covers pulled up to her chin all seemed uncommonly normal when it was standing in the room.

It was immediately next to the pillows, not five inches away. Although it was because she was lying on her back, it still seemed to tower above her - she couldn't see its face. A white figure, dressed in a long gown, indistinct; blurred at the edges. It stood, mute, for what seemed like hours. Carol felt that if she could only move, she would snap out of the dream, so slowly she raised her head.

She didn't wake.

Her movement seemed to spur the thing on; it began to bend with nocturnal deliberation, the place where its face should be coming level with hers...Carol squeezed her eyes shut and listened to the thunder of her blood and her own voice saying,

"I know why you're here... I'm sorry. I'm so sorry. I know what she did."

***

Carol's no stranger to haunting. The other time Carol saw a ghost, she really only saw its footsteps. Walking through the cemetery she looked back and saw footprints indenting in the deep drifts of brittle autumn leaves, following her own path. She carried on walking, watching them follow behind, the quick little footsteps. She felt no fear at all. When she told Dave, he reasoned that it was the leaves settling again in her own foot-holes, and she agreed. Privately, she knew the history of that place. The history of the cemetery. The cemetery where they buried Ben.

***

Carol met David at university. In 1984 it was still exciting to be studying there, Carol in her red tights, in her own room, watching *The Young Ones* on her tiny portable television with her Chinese boyfriend. She felt exotic. A year later, they graduated. Then, two years after that they got married. Things seemed to happen to a pattern back then, just slotted into place. Modern life seemed to be losing that pattern; things happening out of order.

They got married in a register office in spring and that was just fine. Dave's mum moved the white lilies from the desk and put her own pot of peonies in their place, blazing. Carol got nervous giggles when she had to sign her new name, 'Carol Song,' like a hymn. She liked being a Song. Dave's parents were wonderful to her. His dad, Song Nianzu, he was known as Charlie and was quite happy to be a Westerner. Dave's mum Fan Xingjuan spoke Mandarin in front of strangers and refused to cook Yorkshire pudding, but she was happy all the same with the registry office. Then when Charlie died, she covered all the mirrors in the house and wouldn't let Carol take Ben for a haircut for months afterwards. She would always say "Ben will meet a nice girl at university, just like David."

But Ben didn't go to university.

On the night of the accident, nobody could sleep. Next door's dog howled past midnight and Dave turned his face into the pillows, groaning,

"Somebody make them shut that bloody thing up."

Carol got up to make a cup of chocolate and passing the doorway of the lounge she recoiled, seeming to see a figure seated in the dark. There was someone there. Mother Fan had pulled open the curtains and was staring intently out at the street-lit road, waiting. Carol said, "You don't have to wait up for Ben, you know. He's sharing a taxi home with Craig Roper."

And Mother Fan said, "He's not coming home."

***

THE GRAVEYARD EDITION

On the day of Ben's funeral, Mother Fan draped all the mirrors again. Carol put mini-quiches into the fridge and felt numb. The boys had spent all of their taxi fare on beer and had tried to walk home the short way, cutting across the dual carriageway. It was there that Ben had been hit by a van going seventy. At the hospital, Craig Roper's eyes had been swollen shut from crying and it was Carol he couldn't stop saying sorry to. She'd hugged him, and he'd started crying again.

They'd walked over dry grass to the gravesite. In the 1930's, the council had moved a load of very old graves from there, to make room for new ones. The old ones from the 1600's or earlier without headstones, their occupants long forgotten: they had too many tenants. In several of the plots, bags had been found, buried shallowly at the foot of the grave, holding the bones of children.

It was poor parents whose children died and who couldn't afford plots in the overcrowded city cemeteries that would steal into the churchyard at night and bury their children at the foot of existing graves. So they would be interred in holy ground. So they would be safe.

Even to the present day, people heard children singing and talking there. Things had been seen.

Carol wondered how anyone could bring themselves to dig up a grave, to place another body secretly in there with the dead; you must have to be so certain that you're doing it for good. It was the 4th of July and somewhere across the ocean, America was celebrating. 'Four' in Chinese sounds close to the word 'death'. Nobody should have to bury their only child.

At the first rainstorm patter of earth on the casket lid, the mourners turned to depart, a tide of retreating black with Mother Fan weaving between them, tight-lipped in white. The wake was held back at David and Carol's house; condolences and small talk and people hesitating in doorways clutching plates and paper napkins. Excuses for hasty goodbyes and strained, flat laughter that was 'what he would have wanted.' And Carol didn't have to take care to not go straight home straight away in case the ghost of the departed followed her there from the wake, because she was already home, and they were already haunted.

***

"Ben is lonely."

Carol; up to her elbows in hand washing. She wrung out a bra, draping it over the draining board and turned around, drying her hands on the checked tea towel.

"Ben is lonely," said Mother Fan, "He came into my room last night and told me so."

Her eyes were serious. Carol shook her head, carried on drying her dry hands on the towel.

"Mum, Ben is gone…"

"Ben is lonely! No good burying him without a wife,"

"He was just eighteen…"

"No good for him or us! He is lonely. He needs a wife."

"No, mum."

"He needs a Ghost Bride."

Carol dropped the towel and bent to retrieve it, twisting it in her fists.

"I know that tradition is important to you, mum. But Ben is dead. My son is dead." She sobbed once, like a gasp of shock. Her mother-in-law turned and left the room, although from beyond the kitchen door, a faint, muttered 'lonely' could be heard.

***

They were two boys from the same university Ben would've gone to. Mother Fan paid them, just one hundred pounds each. It was cheap, ridiculously cheap, but then it had to beat minimum wage bar work, or volunteering for medical research since the government had stopped student grants.

One of the boys was tall and rake-thin, with a diagonal wedge of over-dyed black hair and woefully bad skin. The other was small and Chinese, with long hair and a metal bar that went straight through two parts of his ear. He looked nervous. It was the Chinese boy that Mother Fan gave all her instructions to, even though he could only speak English and had a strong Lancashire accent.

She didn't know where they'd got her from. Girls were killed to procure Ghost Brides. Mother Fan suspected that this one had been dug up, or smuggled from a student training lab somewhere. It didn't matter. It was best not to know.

It was an inauspicious time for a marriage - late July, the Season of the Hungry Ghost. It could hardly be helped. The moon was a high, sharp sickle and cast little light. The thin boy hefted a spade and strode between the stones with an air of familiarity, his torch a little yellow full moon slipping across the swags of carved ivy that adorned the Victorian monuments - ivy for marriage, ivy for death. The smaller boy carried a large roll of fabric and shook. His face in the gloom was drained white. Wisps of long, black hair drifted from one end of the bundle in his arms. Mother Fan said, "Stop. Here."

The circle of torchlight came to rest on white marble. The headstone read 'BEN YONGNIAN SONG. 12 September 1989 – 26 June 2007.

Dearly missed.' Mother Fan said, "Now."

The marriage was conducted secretly, no proposal, no birthday matching, no bride-price or wedding gifts. Mother Fan gave thanks and respect to the universe and the ancestors. At her indication, the boy carrying the bundle of red fabric stooped to lower it into the shallow pit before the headstone. The body felt light, desiccated and gave off a strange, faint smell like grapefruit; sweet and bitter. The red silk veil covering her face like blushing Nuwa fell away as they rolled her into the shallow hole: lucky red gave way to sorrowful white; her eyes white, rolled back in their sockets and half open, her lips shrunken, drawn back in a somehow-smile from her bright little teeth. Her frail hands like white lotus flowers, the fingers curled.

Mother Fan crouched down and dropped a bunch of yellow roses in. She hadn't been able to find peonies or orchids at short notice. Standing, she pulled from her pocket a lai-see envelope filled with paper money, and a copper coin. She tossed them into the grave.

The boys' torch shone into the hole, reflecting off the lucky mirror fastened to the Bride's skirt and sending wheels of light carouselling around the earth walls of the grave. Lingering about that little shell was the impression that in life she must have been very beautiful, or very terrible. The Chinese boy said, in a whisper, "Her name is Tian Jing."

Mother Fan gave him a long, questioning look. The first shovelful of soil fell from the thin boy's spade and sprayed across the Bride's sightless eyes.

***

"Mum, what have you done?"

The question came out a lot louder than Carol had intended, more accusatory. She'd caught Mother Fan just leaving the house and called after her. The old woman stopped in the doorway, one slim, brown hand on the handle, but she didn't turn around.

"What do you mean?"

The tone of her voice dared Carol to carry on. Carol said, softly, "I know what you've done."

"What have I done?"

It was almost as if she was testing to see if Carol really knew. It was frustrating, this call and response over an act so sober.

"You know what I'm talking about, you know very well and so do I. Dave says the grave's been disturbed. Squirrels, or birds, or kids even – that's what he said…"

She paused. Then, "Who was she?" Carol, tear-glaze washing her view, "That poor, poor girl. She was someone's daughter for God's sake, someone's sister maybe! Where did she come from? Did you kill her?"

At this, Mother Fan finally turned around. Not outraged, but outrageously calm. She said,

"Nobody was killed."

"Then why is she visiting me every night?"

Carol's voice was loud now and the tears tumbled over and crawled down her cheeks. Mother Fan walked back to her, neat economical steps, and patted her arm. Carol; exhausted. Mother Fan smiled.

"So you do see her! Ben tells me, the wedding was all wrong. His wife did not meet you and this troubles her. She needs your blessing before they rest."

***

Carol went to the cemetery that night without really questioning it. She thought she'd feel foolish, but all she felt was nervous to freezing point.

The onward night had cooled the air, but the breeze was still surprisingly warm, with that summer night time sweetness. The sky was saturated blue-black. All the buildings she passed looked flat and oddly lit as film-set backdrops.

Carol thought of the dead, snug down there in their narrow houses. She retraced her steps of a few weeks ago through sweeping grass cloudy with dandelion clocks, until she found the patted-down earth of Ben's grave.

It really just looked like a new grave. Not tampered with at all. The soil was bare, true, with a few grass shoots coming through and a faux-marble urn filled with ox-eye daisies. The letters on the urn stood out; brassy, cheerful, golden. Ben. So obviously new next to the neighbouring urn's green streaks of sleepy verdigris.

Carol knelt beside the plot. She found herself patting down the ground as if she were tucking sheets. Tucking him in, for the last time, now – a married man can look after himself. Time to let go. Carol said, "You have my blessing. Please – take good care of each other."

Shapes like the fleeing shadows outlined by car headlamps across the monuments: two large shapes (cast you'd have thought by arched headstones) that looked like a couple holding hands; several littler figures that could have been the stretched shadows of flower urns or could have been centuries-ago children dancing between them. The sound of the breeze through dried-out flower stems and faded paper windmills, like the rustling of fast footsteps, like the wheeling in the air of a thousand souls taking flight.

EZABELL FROWNED
Melissa J. Davies

Ezabell frowned as she heard wheels crunch on the gravel of the driveway; she hated visitors. She hated them walking around, looking at things. Her things. They talked loudly, with horrible harsh accents and their funny foreign languages. She hated them.

Ezabell knew that Nanny said they were a good thing, these visitors. That they paid money to walk around and look at her belongings. She knew that the money they paid went towards making the castle better. The money had paid to fix part of a ceiling that had fallen down and replace a corner of carpet in the Great Hall.

Ezabell was grown up enough to know that this was a very important thing. But she still hated them. She wondered if she had time to go and see if Nanny was in the kitchen before the visitors arrived at the front door. Normally at this time of day the kitchen would be alive with the sounds and smells of food preparation, pots clanging and the persistent thud of the meat cleaver carving through joints being readied for the evening meal. But the kitchen had been quiet for some time, Ezabell frowned as she tried to remember the last time she had heard those sounds and smelt those smells. Ezabell wondered where Nanny was, it seemed to her that it had been a long time since she had seen Nanny.

The sight of the visitors disembarking the vehicle, talking, laughing and taking pictures made her stop her foray into the kitchens, perhaps she didn't have time after all and needed to make herself scarce in order to remain unseen.

Ezabell frowned as the visitors made their way through the front doors and gathered in the entrance hall. She could hear them talking, exclaiming how old and beautiful the castle was. She frowned as the tour guide started talking, explaining the history of the castle and the legends that surrounded it.

Ezabell listened as the tour guide went on to describe the so-called hauntings that had occurred, that people had reported seeing a young boy dressed in blue darting between rooms and playing with other children. How when the bones of a man and small boy had been found in the wall the bones were buried and the reported activity lessened, as if the boy had found peace. Ezabell always wondered what had happened to the man, why it was only the boy that was seen, or allowed himself to be seen.

Ezabell knew that people paid to come here and liked to feel frightened, but she knew it was rubbish. The castle was not haunted, especially not by a boy whose bones had been in the wall. She listened as the tour guide explained how workers had found the remains of the man and the boy; how the boy's finger bones and nails had been broken as if he had tried to claw his way out, to escape his prison with his bare hands. The visitors loved that part, the poor boy entrapped; his screams muffled by the 10-foot stonewall. Ezabell frowned as the guide went on to talk about the so-called White Pantry Ghost who apparently roams around the kitchens asking for water, appearing to a soldier when the castle was used a hospital during the war. The poor soldier was reported to be too frightened to spend another night in the castle. Ezabell couldn't understand why a pantry maid could not fetch her own water or why a pantry maid would ask a soldier for help or what sort of a soldier would be frightened off by a pantry maid. Ezabell did not believe that this ghost walked the castle either.

Shaking her head, Ezabell left the narrow gallery above the hall, deciding to continue her spying once the group reached the Great Hall, the huge old fireplaces were perfect for hiding in.

She knew that Nanny would shout at her if she were seen, so she crept along the wall of the gallery to remain completely out of sight. She knew all the ways round the castle; she could creep about, unseen, as much as she wanted to. She knew the gaps in the walls and the secret stairways. She knew the tapestries that she could hide behind and the doors she could open silently.

Ezabell crept along the wall of the gallery until she reached the Great Hall. Once there, Ezabell climbed into the enormous stone fireplace. She hopped up into the small nook that was just big enough for her to sit on, her legs tucked under her. From this spot she could hear the visitors but they would not be able to see her, even if they looked right up the fireplace. She loved knowing that she could follow the visitors around the castle, from room to room without them ever knowing she was there. She liked that it made them feel like they were being watched, that perhaps there was some truth in the ghost stories. When of course it was just her; Ezabell, always watching, listening, making sure they didn't touch anything or take any of her belongings. She hated it when the visitors touched her things. There were signs of course, telling people not too, but they still did. Ezabell hated that. She thought about the last time she had spotted a visitor taking something. A woman, who was quite frankly old enough to know better, had tried to take a brass candlestick from the dining table in the Banquet Room. Ezabell had made sure the woman regretted her theft. Ezabell had made sure the woman had put her candlestick back. She hated it when the visitors thought they could just take her things without her knowing.

She heard the group approach the Great Hall, speaking in soft, hushed tones. The guide was explaining about the history of the hall, about the family that lived in the castle all those years ago. Ezabell frowned, she hated hearing those names, the castle was hers, not theirs. The tour guide moved to the next room and Ezabell climbed down from her hiding spot. The next room was what the guide referred to as the James' 1st Room, named after a visit from the King himself, but Ezabell didn't like to call it that, she called it the ceiling room. As she made her way silently along the corridor, she realized that one of the visitors had broken from the group and was sitting on a chair. Ezabell frowned. The chairs were not for visitors to sit on.

The visitor was playing with something; a white box that Ezabell didn't recognize, it was making strange noises that Ezabell couldn't understand.

She inched closer to the visitor, creeping closer and closer until she was so close she could smell him, he smelt of fresh air and washing powder. The visitor carried on playing; unaware that Ezabell was so close.

"Come with me" she whispered.

The visitor carried on playing, as if he hadn't heard her.

"Come with me" she whispered again.

The visitor looked up, startled. Ezabell jumped back. A female voice called out, the boy leapt up as if he had been caught doing something he shouldn't have been doing and rushed off, back into the ceiling room.

Ezabell frowned.

She followed the visitor into the ceiling room, making sure she was silent and unnoticed. Finding her hiding hole, she kept watch, this time only watching the boy.

Nanny had warned her about speaking to the visitors; she knew she was not allowed to speak to them. The visitors were there to provide money, to fix the things that needed fixing; they were not to be disturbed while they were doing the castle tour. There was a leak Nanny said, that needed to be seen to. They were not to be spoken to. Ezabell was to keep away and not play any of her tricks. Nanny didn't approve of Ezabell's tricks.

Ezabell knew that if Nanny found out that she had tried to speak to one of the visitors she would get into trouble, but Ezabell thought that it might only be if she tried to speak to the adult visitors, she thought that it might be allowed for her to speak to a child visitor.

The group had left the room, she knew the route the guide would take them, down the long hall, down the stairs to the entrance hall and then left.

Down the cold stairs they would go, to the place that Ezabell hated. As much as she hated the visitors, as much as she wanted to spy on them and make sure they didn't touch anything, she would not follow them down there. She would not go with them into the room with the scratches on the walls and the deep, dark pit. The pit where bones lay bare, lonely. The bones of a girl child still visible; lost long ago, now lying in the cold dark room surrounded by iron and black. To be gawped at by the visitors.

Ezabell hated that most of all.

The visitors descended the steps, coming to a stop just inside the dungeon doorway. They listened to the tour guide in silent horror as it was described how the prisoners were held and tortured. How cages of starving rats were attached to a prisoner's stomach, leaving the rats no choice but to eat their way out - through their victims. The spiked barrel that was used by securing a man inside, then the barrel was rolled round and around until his flesh was torn off.

But by far, the most chilling aspect of this room was the skeleton of a young girl, the last person to be thrown down the oubliette. Her hollow unseeing eyes staring back at the visitors, following them around the room, sending a shiver down the spine of even the most courageous. The guide was always unable to ask the inevitable questions about who she was and why she had found her final resting place in this way, why a young girl had been amongst all this evil and torture. Why she was the last life to end this way, if in fact she had been the last to endure this horror or whether it had taken a different form.

No, Ezabell would not go there, she would not go down to that dark place that frightened her so much. The place where The Dark Man still reigned, installing his evil into the walls around him.

She knew that the tour guide would take them out of the dark place, up the cold stairs, back to the entrance hall. From there the group would be allowed to walk around the grounds unguided, sometimes visitors would picnic by the lake.

Ezabell would watch them from the castle, to make sure they picked up after themselves. Always watching.

Ezabell wandered back into the ceiling room, she liked it in there. She felt safest when she was surrounded by her favourite things, the tapestries on the walls, the ornate chairs but most of all she liked the ceiling. She would lie on the carpeted floor and stare at the ceiling, her eyes following the gilding all the way along to the moulded pendants and back again. She would wait here until she heard the soft sound of movement below, signaling the visitors were returning to the entrance hall.

Out of the silence, she heard a low thud, the sound of a shoe on stone.

She jumped up from her resting place and hid behind the largest tapestry, the wall curved inwards there and the thick rough material of the tapestry provided just enough space for Ezabell's thin frame. It was the young boy visitor. He should not be in this room; he should be downstairs or outside but certainly not here. She peeked out at him; he was shuffling around, as if he was looking for something. He looked young, not as young as Ezabell but not that much older. He was small, slight and pale.

Ezabell frowned; she wondered what he was looking for. She whispered, "Come with me."

The boy looked up. He shivered, he felt cold all of a sudden.

"Come with me," she whispered again. The hair on the boy's arm stood up, the feeling of someone walking on his grave unnerved him.

The boy turned his head; unable to place where the sound was coming from.

"Come with me," louder this time, more insistent.

The boy stepped forward, towards Ezabell, trying to locate where the words were coming from. She was still behind the tapestry, not wanting to reveal her hiding place yet.

"Come with me."

The boy looked straight at the tapestry. She peered out.

"Hello?" His voice small and nervous.

Ezabell peered out at him.

"Oh, hello!" The boy said, cheerful now. "Are you with the tour as well? I don't think you're supposed to be in here. I was told off earlier for walking off. I didn't see you with the group."

"Come with me." Ezabell said again, louder than a whisper but still barely audible.

"Yeah, ok. Where're we gonna go?" The boy said.

"Come with me," she said and ran from the room, hoping the boy would follow.

The boy stood in the room for a moment, knowing he should go and find his mum and dad but he was bored of the boring castle. He followed Ezabell, even though he didn't quite know what to think of this strange girl who made him feel a bit odd, a bit nervous.

She seemed to have vanished, the boy was confused for a minute, not understanding how she was there one minute and gone the next. He supposed that there must be loads of secret passageways and hidden doors in the castle, but he didn't really know how this girl knew about them, or why she was there. She definitely hadn't been with the tour group and the guide had said that no one lived in the castle anymore. The family was long gone and the castle was owned by the Trust.

From where Ezabell was standing she could see the confusion on the boy's face, she whispered, "Come with me."

He looked, startled. She was standing right in front of him.

She ran off, making sure this time that the boy was following her. She ran to the end of the hallway, to the enormous fireplace. Once there, she jumped. The boy stopped, confused. He followed her into the fireplace; he was not as nimble or as quick as she was. He looked up and saw Ezabell on a small ledge, then she disappeared. He jumped, grabbing onto a crack in the wall and managed to swing his way up onto the ledge. He gasped as it became clear that the ledge was leading to a tiny stone staircase. He tried to run up the steps, catching a glimpse of Ezabell's blue dress as she turned a corner. Stumbling a couple of times on the uneven slabs, he had to steady himself on the rough surface of the walls.

Ezabell reached the top of the stairs and frowned. He had followed her. Pushing the heavy wooden trap door up and across she revealed the rooftop. She frowned as the sun hit her face, getting in her eyes, although the air was cold and the sky was overcast Ezabell was unused to being outside. She did not make a habit of leaving the castle, unless it was to spy on the visitors. Pulling herself up and out, she was on the roof, the turrets tall on either side of her. From here she could see almost all of the grounds, the Royal Gardens, the lake, all the way to the woods. If she looked hard enough she would see some of the cattle that roamed, still wild after all these years. But now was not the time to be looking at cows or woods. The boy had caught up with her; he stared at her as if he didn't understand what she was doing, why she had insisted that he follow her up here. He wasn't sure if she had in fact insisted, or if he wanted to. There was something strange about that, he couldn't understand why he had followed her.

She looked pale in the weak sunlight, almost transparent. She stared back.

"What are we doing up here? Who are you? Why won't you tell me your name?"

These questions made Ezabell nervous. She wasn't used to speaking to anybody except for Nanny, let alone a visitor. She chose not to answer him yet. There would be plenty of time for answering questions later, after.

She started to move closer to the edge, slowly.

"Come with me," she whispered.

The boy looked at her, not understanding where the impulse was coming from, and yet he stepped forward.

"Come with me," she whispered again.

The boy stepped further forward.

The boy blinked and Ezabell was on the edge of the parapet, sitting with her legs dangling over the edge. He couldn't quite understand how she had managed to get up there so quickly, without a sound.

"Come with me," she whispered.

The boy grasped the parapet next to her, hauling himself up.

"I'm scared," he said. "I don't like being up this high."

Ezabell frowned.

The boy carried on. "I think my Mum will be wondering where I am. I should go back. I don't think I should be here. I want to go and find my Mum."

Ezabell frowned.

The boy felt calmer then. He didn't know how or why but he wasn't scared anymore. He thought he rather liked being up there after all. He liked to see all the trees and the birds flying. He noticed a hawk hovering above some unseen prey in the field below, about to dart down. He felt happy then, like he wanted to stay up here with Ezabell. All thoughts of his family or finding his mother were gone. All he thought about now was staying up here and being with Ezabell.

"Come with me," she whispered again, sensing that the boy's state of mind had changed. There was a shift in the air around them. Ezabell frowned.

The boy stood up, then, his foot slipped on a piece of moss. He tried to grasp hold of the parapet, of Ezabell, of anything. But there was nothing.

The boy fell, no noise escaped from him. He fell in silence, landing with a hollow thud on the ground below. His back twisted, grotesque.

Ezabell looked down on the boy's motionless body.

At last she was no longer alone; Ezabell smiled.

THE VIEWING
Lance Davis

Andrew clutched the letter that began with the words: "We regret to inform you," and ended with directions to the funeral home that now held the body of his uncle Dwayne. Sweat trickled down his face as he contemplated turning around and going home, his new girlfriend sensed his hesitation.

"Andrew," she urged, "you've come this far, you might as well see it through."

"But I didn't really know him Tess, no one did." He looked at the double white painted doors before him. "Nobody's going to be here anyway."

He had already gone over this with her. Told her how his uncle was a drunk loner, a drug abuser, rumored to be a thief and possibly worse. "And you certainly didn't have to come," he finished, reluctantly striding up beside her.

"Believe me Andrew, I want to be here."

She urged him forward and together they marched to the waiting doors, above which hung a simple hand painted sign that proclaimed this to be Thatcher Funeral Home.

He grasped the cool brass knob and pushed. A blast of cold air escaped and embraced him. Tess tightened her grip and encouraged him to enter. After the physical shock of stepping outside the humid July heat and into this large wooden freezer, he was attacked with a mental shock of seeing so many people. None of the strangers turned to acknowledge them.

"More people here than I thought," he whispered. "I didn't see any vehicles."

"Maybe they're local."

"Local? We didn't pass a house for miles."

She shrugged and pulled him onward toward the simple wooden casket at the front of the room. He pulled back.

"Let's just take a seat back here," he suggested, leading her to a secluded pew at the back of the room.

Something more than the obvious dead body of his uncle in the room was bothering him. He rubbed his hands against his legs both from nervousness and for warmth. It was so intensely cold his fingers were feeling numb. He studied the strangers seated randomly in front of them to take his mind off it.

A few rows up and to their left sat a young brown haired girl and a middle aged man who looked to be her father. A row in front of them and to their right sat a young man in a leather motorcycle jacket. Various others were scattered about. All heads were bowed. He finally figured out what was bothering him.

"It's so quiet," he whispered.

Now that he had noticed it, it was almost overwhelming how silent it was. There were no hushed whispers or quiet sobs. All were solemn. Their attention seemed entirely focused on whatever was on the hardwood floor directly in front of them.

A slim woman, Andrew guessed maybe mid-fifties, suddenly stood and approached the casket. For a moment she merely stared at the open coffin. Then slowly, she walked around and faced the crowd.

Her long curly brown hair draped over her face, nearly covering her dark brown eyes, and when she spoke her voice was just as dark.

"You all know why we are here today," she began, "not to mourn, nor to celebrate the passing of this man."

She paused and heads nodded their agreement in unison.

"But to take," she continued, "what is ours."

Andrew felt a chill go down his back. He looked at Tess with confusion.

"What's she talking about?" he whispered.

Tess only nodded from left to right and continued to look forward. Andrew waited for the stranger to continue, and when she did, her voice had gained momentum.

"We have all been affected in one way or another by Dwayne Benjamin Lewis. The lives we had, all harmed at the hands of this one man."

Heads nodded more vigorously than before, mumbled voices joined in. The crowd was getting worked up and still, she continued. "Nobody cared for this soul, and rightfully so. Who could possibly care for a soul that cared for no one? He had no friends and no one he cared to call family."

Her eyes landed on Andrew and he could swear he saw a flicker of a smile. He was getting angry.

"She can't say that," he whispered to Tess, who simply looked at him.

The stranger continued her sermon.

"You Jake," she pointed at the guy in the motorcycle jacket. "You were his partner in a drug deal that went wrong for you, were you not?"

The man nodded.

"And you David," she pointed to the man with the young girl, "didn't he harm your daughter one drunken night?"

He nodded in agreement.

"I, too, was robbed and beaten by this man."

Once again, her eyes landed on Andrew. "It's no wonder his only living relative is too ashamed to come forward and pay his respects."

Andrew's anger and confusion had reached its peak. He quickly stood.

"What is going on?" he demanded, starting up the aisle. "Who are you anyway?"

He could feel heads and eyes turning on him, but he was locked on the lady. Her smile only continued to grow.

"You were outside that night. Weren't you Andrew?"

He stopped mid-aisle.

"What night?"

She laughed. The sound of it made him cringe as it echoed throughout the room.

"The night you heard the gunshot," she answered.

He was frozen to the floor.

"Perhaps," she continued, "if you had come inside with him you would know who I am."

Andrew was suddenly rocked with memories of a night he had spent his life trying to forget. Among the chaos that stampeded through his brain, he heard her say a name.

"Elise Thatcher."

"That's impossible," he whispered.

Everything suddenly seemed like a dream. The sound of his breathing was amplified. He lifted his concrete laden foot and took a step forward, the fall of it thundered throughout the room. He had an overwhelming urge to see his uncle's body, and she waited. His eyes, locked on hers, never wavering. Finally, he reached her, the casket between them.

"What are you afraid of?" she asked.

His hands gripped the hard wood sides of the open top. The tips of his fingers slid into the open mouth of the coffin, immediately, they felt wet and sticky. He pulled them out and up to his face. Red liquid dripped from his fingertips. He could deny it no longer and cast his eyes downward.

The coffin was full of blood. The bruised and beaten almost unrecognizable face of his uncle just protruded from the gore. Andrew began to shake violently.

"I'm losing my mind," he said to himself as his uncle's eyes slid open to gaze at him. The jaw flexed in an attempt to speak but no sound emerged.

Andrew's paralysis broke and he whirled away from the sight to find Tess standing at the back door and all eyes in the room staring at him. Before he could move, Elise Thatcher's claw-like hand gripped his shoulder and dug in, her nails breaking the skin.

"My daughter won't help you," Elise whispered.

"She's your mother?" he wailed at Tess, who continued to stand with her back to the door.

"You knew about all this?" he continued.

Finally, she spoke, "I knew you were there when he killed my mother," she paused, and the room was silent, "and if there are others here, I can't see them."

"What do you mean you can't see them?"

She smiled. "Because, they're not here for me Andrew, they're here for you."

The faces and bodies of the strangers about the room began to change. Some began bleeding from unseen holes, bodies contorted into various postures of agony. The young girl fell to the floor and began to pull herself up the aisle toward him, her legs mangled. Her father, with a freshly formed bullet hole in his head followed her. The young man in the motorcycle jacket, his throat slashed from ear to ear joined him.

"Think of all the lives, including your own, you could have saved had you done things differently that night," Tess finished. She turned and opened the door. Over her shoulder, Andrew could just see the bright summer sunshine and silently begged to be back out in the heat.

"Tess!" he screamed.

He was answered by a slamming door. The bodies of the dead trudged forward and Elise's grip continued to tighten. "We are going to take what is ours," she said to him.

Outside, Tess wandered behind the forsaken building to visit the various shallow graves of missing victims. While inside, the cold continued to plummet and the only thing to escape was a blood curdling scream for help.

THE KEEPER
Nicole DeGennaro

When Donovan opened his eyes, he recognized his surroundings, although he couldn't think from where. Dim light filtered in through the high, gaping holes that windows had once occupied. Mold-laced cracks snaked up the scuffed, stained walls, reaching the ceiling in some spots; underneath the grime lurked the ghost of a soothing shade of blue or perhaps green paint. The skeleton of a drop ceiling and the hollow shells of fluorescent lights hung above him. By the time he climbed off the dingy, stained mattress that sat half on the floor and half on a broken, rusted bedframe, he knew he was in some kind of decrepit, disused hospital. He still didn't know why it looked familiar.

The cold floor chilled his bare feet, and shattered pieces of dirty tile bit at his soles; he glanced down at his clothes, wondering why he was barefoot, and saw he wore a pair of pajama pants and an undershirt. When he looked back up, something moved in the darkness just beyond the broken, half-open door. The urge to flee seized him.

He crept forward, doing his best to avoid the debris scattered on the floor. The only way out was through the door, and he pushed it open further, expecting it to creak. Despite being off one hinge, it swung outward without a sound. He stuck his head out and peered into the semidarkness but saw no hint of an exit; the light that leaked into the room barely reached the hallway, which had none of its own windows. Motionless, mysterious shapes he couldn't identify loomed in the murk. Still, his gut told him to bolt.

He stepped out of the room and turned right, running his hand along the wall to give himself a point of reference as he moved down the hall. Paint flaked away under the light touch of his fingers; sometimes bits of drywall crumbled when he disturbed an old gash. As he peered around, some of the motionless shapes became recognizable as the corpses of abandoned hospital equipment and deteriorated building materials. He toed around broken wheelchairs and rotting wood, but the smaller things he stumbled on remained unidentifiable. The stale air stank of damp and mold, and it settled deep in his lungs. As he slunk down the hall, the sense of being hunted made his hair stand on end, although he heard nothing but his own breathing.

His fingers sank into something slimy and he recoiled, wiping his hand on the hem of his shirt. As he moved away from the wall, he stepped on something that deflated with a small pop, releasing a warm puff of air. The foul odor of putrefaction made him gag, as if he had burst a bag containing the stench of an animal long decayed. The sound of his retching filled the hall; when it faded he froze in place, his heart giving an apprehensive flutter as he waited for something to pounce on him from the darkness. Nothing came for him.

He continued forward, staying close to the wall but no longer touching it. After what felt like hours of walking, he reached the end of the hall to discover it branched into another, gloomier corridor. Seeing no exit signs, Donovan made a guess and went to the left.

As he turned the corner, something crashed behind him, and the sound of hurried footsteps echoed down the hall. He broke into a jog, the almost total darkness keeping him from a full-out run. He stumbled over more debris, too focused on his frantic search for a way out to worry about obstacles or keeping quiet. His hands pawed the damaged walls; he could not feel or see a single door or window. With rising dread he realized he had turned down a dead end. He came to a stop and held his breath, straining to hear any indication of his pursuer, but the frenzied beating of his blood-engorged heart deafened him. The tang of adrenaline stung the back of his throat.

He took a deep breath and spun around, almost hoping whatever was hunting him would make its move, free him from his terror. Instead, only the ominous, indeterminate specters of debris populated the corridor. Nothing moved. Could he have imagined the footsteps he had heard? He groped back the way he had come, again using the wall as a reference despite the earlier incident. When he reached the opening to the hall he had started in he continued past it, wanting to see what was down the other end of the smaller corridor; within a minute he reached another dead end.

"Damn it," he said, the words devoured by a loud bang from somewhere behind him. As he turned and pressed his back against the wall, he cringed at the harsh sound of metal scraping against the floor. He stared into the darkness and watched as a figure emerged from the larger hallway. Its silhouette had the general shape of a person, but Donovan couldn't discern anything else. Its undulating form stood out against the gray-black murk, as if all light fled from its presence—as if it were composed of pure nothingness.

He slapped his right hand over his mouth to stifle any sounds that might slip out, smearing remnants of the slimy substance on his cheek. He tried to ignore the strange sour taste on his lips from his dirty fingers and the faint excremental scent from the gunk. All he could do was hope the creature would turn the other way first. That might give him a chance to find an exit. The shape stood motionless for what could have been days, for what felt like weeks; then, finally, the creature turned and headed away from him, fading into the gloom. Still, Donovan paused—if he didn't wait long enough he might run into it, but if he waited too long it would come back—then he dropped his hand, sucked in a breath and set off at a dead run, making for the larger hallway. At least if he couldn't find the exit he could return to the room to hide. Anything had to be better than the corridor of dead ends. When he bolted around the corner he kicked something metal that clanged across the floor; the noise bounced off the crumbling walls and shook his bones.

He sped up as something skittered behind him. In his haste he raced past the door to the room and then slipped on some kind of puddle on the floor. Once he regained his balance he kept running as best as he could with a wet, sticky coating on the bottom of his right foot. The creature let out a horrifying shriek, sending a spasm through Donovan's body. He glanced over his shoulder—the shape was closer than he thought, gliding toward him like oil, slick and viscous. He turned away, trying to move faster, dodging around obstacles, and in the dimness he saw it: an exit sign, hanging over a door at the far end of the hall. Bright, yellow-white light seeped through the gaps between the door and its frame; he was certain neither the sign nor the door had been there earlier, but he didn't care. He could make it if he pushed himself a little harder.

A sharp piece of rubble ripped his left foot open, and with a cry of pain he tumbled to the ground. He collided with an abandoned, broken wheelchair, which screeched as it slid with him across the floor.

Blood dripped from his foot, and he did his best not to put the open wound down on the dirty floor. Spots of white flashed across his vision from the pain. He could get back up, try and hobble along, but he knew he wouldn't reach the exit. Instead, he hid himself behind the wheelchair and a nearby bed lying on its side, doing his best to form a makeshift shelter.

The oily shape solidified as it closed the distance, knocking bedframes and other wreckage out of its way instead of moving around them. It made a persistent, unsettling noise as it approached—giggling. The creature was giggling. A spike of fear stabbed Donovan's heart and froze his blood.

"I seeeeeee youuuuuuu," it called, and Donovan shuddered as he recognized the voice. Panic seized him; he tried to scuttle away but hit the wheelchair. He was sure he was going to die there, four yards from freedom.

She stopped in front of the bed, then reached forward with one hand and pushed it aside. It sailed across the hall and crashed into the opposite wall. Donovan decided he didn't want to die curled up in a terrified ball, so with all his weight on his slick but uninjured right foot, he stood up to face his sister.

"Found you," she hissed, taking another step toward him. Her brown hair hung in thick, greasy clumps over her grime-smeared face, which glistened with sweat and possibly blood. Her torn clothes clung to the pointed joints of her body. Donovan wanted to stand firm, but he instinctively limped backward. She giggled.

"Hester," he choked out, terror tightening his throat. His sister cocked her head to one side, as if she recognized the name but didn't know why, and then her mouth cracked into a huge, wicked grin like a chainsaw, full of sharp, tearing points. A sound escaped him, something between a moan and a cry, and then Hester lunged at him.

Donovan put his hands up and waited for the impact. It never came. After a minute, he opened his eyes and glanced around. The soothing green walls surrounded him on all sides, no cracks to be seen. A clean, complete drop ceiling floated above him, the tiles interspersed with inactive fluorescent lights. Moonlight glimmered down from the barred, unreachable but intact windows, lending everything a calming glow. He lowered his hands as he regained his bearings, but the return to reality brought him little relief. Everything from the lock on the door to the color of the walls was meant to bring him comfort, offer a sense of safety. Instead, it made him anxious, reminding him that asleep or awake, Hester had him trapped in a nightmare.

DEAR MADAME INSANE
Mathias Jansson

In the strange dwells of the Carpathian woods
the abounded roads to the gates of hell
inside the asylum's serpent's well
trapped inside a circle of salt
with the seal tattooed on my chest
the number of six hundred sixty six

Isolated inside insanity
in solitude screaming
in this endless void of darkness
chained to rusty hooks
crooked in my rotten flesh
until my white temple will be revealed
and finally release my soul
from heaven and hell

The haunted demons
tortures my mind
and scorn me

Dear madam Bathory
you fool who sold your soul
for the pleasure of blood
stay forever with us
in your decaying corpus
we will teach you true pain
and the fame of the insane

THE BASEMENT
K. Trap Jones

A faulty fuse box.

The basis behind my insanity. It was the key determining factor that set in motion a series of events that would ultimately dissect the rational portion of my mind. Fear is objective in a sense, as it differs from person to person, but there is no denying the power that fear holds on an individual. It can shape a personality and instruct their actions. Even when fear is known, even when it is predicted, the mind will never lessen the outcome. As if it cowers in the face of fear, the mind will portray itself as a gladiator, but it will always play the victim. The body merely follows. Without the mind, the body is useless as it can only perform actions that are created and ordered by the mind. But when the mind is rattled to the edge of sanity, the body has no choice but to obey its commands. I grew up in the family business, a funeral home on the outskirts of town. Death was something that was not only forced upon me, but it had become a common factor within my daily life.

As a small child, I was fearless with a free, roaming mind. My thoughts were of action figures and video games, but that would all change. My mother was vacuuming the lobby when I asked her if she had any empty boxes. I was building a fort for the epic battle that was about to take place between *G.I. Joe* and *Star Wars*. She told me that there were plenty in the basement that I could have. Without much thought, I turned on the light and ventured down the stairs. The door swung shut behind me as each step I took produced an eerie sound of the wood bending. The lone swinging light bulb barely provided enough light. The shifting shadows danced amongst the many columns of boxes as if they were playing hide-n-seek. Winding through the boxes like a rat in a maze, I searched for the empty ones. Dust and cob webs produced a grey layer that coated the cardboard. Every cough that I did only added to the thickness of the air. The entire stock of outdated funeral equipment was stored down there. The embalming tubes, canisters and metal tables; everything was thrown down into the basement.

In the back of the darkened room, I found a stack of empty boxes. There was enough to form huge bases for both sides of the war. As I turned around, I quickly realized that the labyrinth of boxes and old caskets became a little more difficult to navigate through, but still I did not have an ounce of nervousness. Seconds; a few seconds was all that needed to alter the path of my life. I heard a faint hissing noise that sounded like a drop of water landing on a hot burner. Then the light went out. Darkness suffocated the basement and completely mutilated my vision. The unforgiving black aura hit me in the back of my head with an iron hammer.

Tears rolled down my face as I screamed out for my mother, but I could hear the vacuum cleaner still powered on. My mind raced in order to stay functional, but the inability to see my own hand directly in front of my face, infected it with madness. The boxes fell from my hand as my pace quickened to find an exit. I collided into the columns causing them to lean over. A feeling of terror was riding upon my neck as I galloped over the dispersed contents, trying desperately to reach the stairs. The darkness became an entity that I could not shake. It was behind me, in front of me and on either side. The worst part was that it was not allowing me to have any breathing room or any safe radius. I felt it teasing me with horrible visions that were scarring my mind and carving through my heart, but I did not stop moving forward. Every foot placement was wrong and my balance suffered the consequences. There were too many obstacles; there was too much darkness.

Fear has a way of shaping a person. Moments earlier, I was a free roaming child trying to build bases for my action figures. In the darkness, I was fighting off death and his grip around my neck was allowing him to win. Turned around in the blackness of the pit, I began to blame my mother and that vacuum cleaner. She was so close to being able to save me, but it felt like cleaning the crumbs off of the floor was more important at the time. My fear turned to anger as the blackened room shifted to a dark red. It was the realization of being helpless in the situation, knowing that there was no one there to help me. Isolation with only death whispering a lullaby proved to be a dagger in my young heart. That damn vacuum cleaner was muffling my screams of panic; it was drowning out my calls for help. I stopped screaming and closed my eyes. The darkness of my eye lids felt more comforting because it was self-inflicted.

With my eyes swollen shut from crying and my throat choked from my unnoticed screams, I heard the vacuum cleaner shut off. Complete silence added to my demise. I hated the vacuum cleaner, but soon realized that the noise had provided me with something to personify with. Silence, on the other hand, brutalized me when I was already weakened. My tongue would not allow me to speak. My buckled knees did not allow me to move. I sat there, swallowing the darkness and dreaming of the light. It felt like eternity before the door opened and the light from the upstairs streamed down the stairs into the basement. My sore eyelids retracted as I squinted and heard the sound of my mother's voice calling my name. I scampered across the overturned boxes as if it were a boneyard. At the base of the stairs, I looked up and saw the silhouette of my mother. I didn't know whether I was glad to see her or not.

Over the next few years, I stayed clear of the basement and tended to the needs of the funeral home. Whatever I wanted that ended up being in that basement, quickly became something that I didn't want anymore. I was never the same after that one encounter with the darkness. My mind began to speak with me as if the darkness had infected my mind. The voices would tell me to do things that I did not want to do. It had me performing patterns in order to fend off its sadistic advances against my sanity. In the moments before falling asleep each night, the darkness crept into my room and hovered above me as I clamored beneath the blankets. My eyes ached from being shut so tight, but I could hear the darkness singing to me. All I wanted was for someone to help me; to understand, but they never did, not friends or family. When I tried to speak, I was always interrupted with their own problems, none of which added up to mine. I was going insane without someone to hear my words, but I was surrounded by people who did not care about how close I was to the line of madness.

Each night, death visited me in the form of the shadows, shifting as the clouds passed over the moon. Fear and pain read me a story each night. They spoke of a young child who was once a strong boy, but became weakened by the thoughts within his own mind. They toyed with my emotions and bullied my thoughts by having me perform ritualistic actions so that death would not visit the ones I loved. Beyond tired, I did as the darkness requested; over and over again until I met the specifications of each demand. Silencing the beast was the only way to regain any ounce of strength so that I could make it through the night. My mind was eroding as the darkness smiled, knowing that I was its slave.

The years continued to roll by as I graduated and took over the funeral home upon the passing of my mother. A new bolt was placed on the basement door. There was no reason for me to venture down there as it would offer me nothing but hardened memories. Through relationships filled heartache I was lured back into that wallowing pit to be helpless against the darkness once again. After a brief period, the darkness had returned and greeted me unconditionally like a long lost friend. I had no more fight within me; I had no more empty boxes to construct a fortified, defensive base. With no help from the ones that claimed to love me or even be my friend, I allowed the darkness to take control. I became a puppet with the blackened voices controlling the strings.

I desired others to feel what I felt. It was what the voices were instructing me to do. Within that moment of helplessness, the darkness became my only friend when everyone else had abandoned me. Left alone, the voices comforted me within my time of need. In my darkest hour, everyone abandoned me, but I was not alone as the shadows of my mind helped me build the defenses so that I could observe the enemy from afar. Everything that was good in my life left me and pushed me into the awaiting arms of my darkened friend who was much too eager to embrace me.

I unlocked the basement door and looked upon the stairs being engulfed by the darkness like stone steps leading down into a murky river. Each step I took down reminded me of those who could have helped me. Every inch of the darkness that crept up my body reminded me of how I had to sit and listen to everyone else as I was forced to bite my own tongue. Each creak of the wooden steps allowed me to reflect upon those who chose to look away and tell me how much they loved me in the same breath. As I descended into the darkened grave, I thought about those who wanted to help others before they would even hear my words. With the black concealing my chest, I intentionally left the light off. I stood on the steps with my body engulfed in the shadows, as it was not an easy decision to fully surrender my soul to the demonic voices within my head. The way I looked at the situation was that everyone within my life had already sacrificed me. With one last breath of the light and a few more tears for the ones that I loved, I donated my sanity to the darkness.

For days, I allowed the basement to swallow me. Chaos had replaced my once calm demeanor. Hatred drained the essence of my once loving heart. Serenity overshadowed the meaningless stress that others pressured me with. I was on the other side of the edge of sanity. I could see myself looking down as I was looking up. I saw the fake ears and lips of those around me. I saw the meaningless people they wanted to help instead of me. I could see concern within their eyes, but I could also see the emotions being directed away from me like they had always done. I witnessed as each of them walked away from the edge and vanish as they tended to those that had wronged them in the past. I had done no such thing. I lived a life of respect and loyalty, but received none in return. Tears flowed down my face as I looked to the edge one last time with the hopes that someone, anyone would extend their hand and help me up. It seemed like eternity as my eyes watched the edge and waited.

My mind informed me that no one was coming; that no one cared. My mind was correct. Throughout my life, my words always fell upon deaf ears. My emotions were cast aside, but there was someone who would now listen and hear my words without speaking their own. There was now someone who would truly be my friend for all the right reasons, who cared about the path that I was on; someone who cared about my wellbeing. Darkness became my only friend and I had come to speak with him. For years I had shunned his voice and ignored his demands, but no longer. What type of friend would I be if I discarded the desires of someone in need? I would be like the others on that ledge looking down. I would not be like them; I would not walk away when someone is pleading for help. I would extend my hand and help them up.

For weeks, I had discussions with the darkness as if it was therapy. He would always listen to me with ears that never judged; with eyes that never wandered. I had never had an outlet such as that before. I would sit within that barren basement spilling my inner most secrets to the shifting shadows that danced upon the stone walls. However, I desired more and the darkness agreed. I needed to be around others who felt the same as I did. I needed an audience that would listen to me without prejudice.

With the help from my true friend, I set in place a plan to create my own support group where the meetings would be held within the basement. I became obsessed with the particulars; tables with snacks, water coolers and chairs formed within a circle. The basement was beautiful with all the fixtures to simulate a therapy group setting. I even had a sign on the basement door that instructed people that they were welcomed to attend. There was only one bullet point left on the list that was left unchecked and that was to invite others to join in.

Over the next few weeks, I began to approach people at the funeral services that I believed would make good attendees and who would really learn from the group. The following meeting, the basement was packed. I was a bit nervous to welcome everyone and had a difficult time swallowing the donut from the snack table. With enough courage, I sat down in my chair with all eyes upon me. I looked across at the nine empty chairs and stared at each of the attendees who were gagged and chained to the basement walls.

In order to help myself, I needed to be around people who felt the same as I did. Unfortunately, I could not find people that fit the characteristics, so I had no other choice but to create the personalities myself. In order to do so, I needed the darkness to first embrace them and inflict fear upon their minds, just like it had done to me.

Step One: Fear of the Unknown

Some of the group members were blazing through the initial step. They were already showing signs of developed madness. Through the relentlessness of the darkness and the sheer brutality of their confinement, I allowed their minds to break down and realize the reality of their situation. A day or so of confinement gifted them each with the concept of fear. That feeling that no one could hear their screams for help above the sound of a vacuum cleaner.

Step Two: Alone

I would talk to each of them individually and remind them that no one knows of their whereabouts. I watched as each of their eyes revealed sadness as their minds understood that they were truly alone or lost within a maze of boxes. It was a feeling of helplessness of not being able to navigate through the darkness and hearing the beast rapidly approaching. I would always leave by casually walking up the stairs. I could sense their eyes watching me as I ascended to the door. I could feel their uneasiness as I slowly shut the door behind me allowing for the light to siphon from the room like a snake in a field of grass.

Step Three: Disappointment

I would offer the concept of disappointment through the cruel use of their malnourishment. I would bring down nine bags of food and drink to the basement and displayed everything on table before them. Their eyes bled with hunger and thirst at the possibility that someone would help them, even just a little. The methodology of hope was always a powerful notion while I was growing up. I always hoped that I would meet someone that would turn my hope into help. Like the others, I would pretend to care and lay out the food as if I was going to feed them. Hope, the single most discouraging factor within someone's life. Hope is nothing more than an internal lie that gets looped within the mind of the weak. I sat and ate one bag of the food so that their eyes could see my expressions while I tasted the hamburger. They could smell the aroma of the French fries. Their muscles flinched in pain as I brought over a garbage can and threw the remaining unopened bags away. There is nothing stronger than disappointment; there is nothing more damaging to a pure soul than to be tossed aside like garbage.

Step Four: Whispers of Death

Within the dead of night, I would sneak into the basement and randomly choose someone. I would whisper the words of death into their ears as they slept. Their involuntary movements informed me that they heard my words, tormenting their already damaged minds. I would weaken their thoughts and dreams by overshadowing the good with the bad. The words planted seeds of corruption within their skulls and dislodged any remnants of sanity that was still lingering about. Their deteriorating minds would never reach the same level of mine, but they would indeed suffer mentally. They began to fear falling asleep as they envisioned the darkness whispering its nightly lullaby. I desired for them to personify with the darkness and embrace the temptations instead of conflicting with it.

Certainly, the most difficult step to instruct. I tried many methods that failed miserably. I found success within the already installed intercom system that I barely used. Sitting upstairs, I was able to bombard them with devastating visions of resentment and despair regardless of whether they were asleep or not. I infested their minds with my words and tried to control their thought patterns. To lose the mind was a blow to the entire makeup of an individual. In order to control the mind, it must first be broken down like a shattered mirror that can eventually be put back together, but the cracks will always remain.

Step Five: Temptation

For not only acknowledging the voices, but listening to them, I would reward them with drink and food. Whatever instructions were embedded within their ears during the previous night, they would welcome me when I arrived with the action or sound. For instance, I whispered the simple command of a dog barking and spoke of ill-spirited consequences if they did not follow the demands. On the other side, I spoke highly of serenity and peace if the demands were met with full acceptance according to the guidelines provided. As soon as the light filtered down the stairs from the opened door, I heard a rush of dogs barking. Some did not listen to the specific instructions and had to start over until the pattern was correct. Self-mental anguish pierced their lungs and crippled their breathing as anxiety crept up their spines and perched itself upon their shoulders. They each knew that the pattern had to be precise in order to reach acceptance. Anything less than perfection would be greeted with failure.

Step Six: Abandonment

I made them feel like they were each standing on the edge of sanity. I saddened their minds with discouraging thoughts and fed them the dissatisfaction of knowing that I was not going to help them. I told them that I planned on keeping them forever and that they all would die within the darkened basement. The reality of being abandoned by the ones you truly loved was what I was trying to push upon them. To be truthfully left alone to deal with a situation that you may never fully understand was a sensation that still plagues me. It all goes back to hope. Hope is a glimmer of a positive outcome that can be seen from a distance. It is a source of power and belief in the good of others. It is the light within the dark that guides someone to a sense of self-worth. However, if there is no light and no one to produce the light, then all that remains is the darkness. With no other option, darkness will get embraced, snuffing out the light permanently. Through days of abandonment training, I believed that I had inflicted enough emotional stress and anxiety within their minds. I could see the sheer sadness within their eyes. There was no more fear; there was no more eagerness to escape. They each embraced the training and passed with flying colors as I saw a little of myself within each of their bloodstained eyes.

The group was successful. Their broken spirits matched my own soul and the damaged emotions that created me as a person. Their shattered minds were tormented to a perfect level to where they would never view the world the same again. They had become an extension of me; we all shared the abolished whispers of death. They no longer moaned in agony when darkness covered them or when my words visited their ears while they slept. A comfort level had been reached, the same that had opened my mind. I had gained a sense of respect for each one of my fellow group members as I truly believed that we all learned a valuable lesson during our daily sessions, but there was one more lesson to be taught; one that I will never learn myself.

Step Seven: Help

Each night, I unchained one person and guided their frail bodies up the stairs away from the constricting darkness. Hooded and handcuffed, they were driven to where I had first encountered them. Once there, I gave them the key and instructed them leave their hoods on until they no longer heard the engine of my car. I told each one to dwell in the extended arm of help that had pulled them up the sharp cliff and lifted them above sanity's ledge.

I felt the appreciation within their demeanors and heard the relief within their cries. I made sure to make it known that they were truly safe now and that they should never lose sight of hope even when those around you try their best to diminish the light by not listening. Step seven served as the greatest gift that anyone would ever do for them. It was a feeling that I so desired for myself, but felt a portion of the relief when I granted it to each of them.

With the last group member released, I stood on the threshold of the basement steps. I was at the crossroads once again. I could certainly lock the door and never go down there again, but without that extended arm to stop me and reassure that everything would be alright, I entered through the door. As I took the first step, I thought about those who loved me and wondered where they had been; whether or not the ones that they were helping were getting better. With the darkness up to my chest, I could hear the whispers swirling around my head. I could feel the shadows pushing me further from behind. Alone, I looked over sanity's edge, not with fear and not with anxiety. I saw the darkness as my home. As everyone else passed me by, I could still grip a small glimmer of hope, that someone, anyone, would offer me a hand.

THAT WHICH REMAINS
Michael Kellar

Specters softly shimmering
In the pale moonlight,
Are said to send a bitter chill
Through those they touch at night.

Yet frigid skeletal fingers
Frantically working their phantom art,
Cannot create a form as cold
As a dark and dismal heart.

I mourn that soft and tender form
Where once my caress was proud,
But will never feel my touch again
For now she wears a silken shroud.

She slipped away far too soon,
After pausing to impart,
The thousand lingering memories
Left to plague my haunted heart.

SINS OF OUR MOTHER
Edward J. McFadden III

Thunder cracked, and clouds hung oppressively low in the heavens, as Jonah walked through the streets of Baltimore with his head down, his hood drawn over his face. He made eye contact with no one, and the dark, rainy street provided the perfect cover. Jonah didn't want to be seen going to the morgue, even though Examiner Raynor would be there, and his presence was perfectly normal given the circumstances. The rain continued to drench him through as he jumped across puddles, his long dark cloak getting sopping wet as it dragged behind him across the dirty cobblestones. Jonah Rybath's mother was dead, and he was on his way to perform the autopsy.

Performing an autopsy on one's own mother violates so many rules of humanity that even in 1949 discovery of such an act would have relegated Jonah to the lowest levels of moral acceptability, but he was an odd man whose eyes and thoughts were forever downward, and he didn't mind taking chances. Aside from the potential legal entanglements, Jonah was a general medical practitioner, and wasn't versed in complicated surgeries or autopsies, yet there were no suspicious circumstances surrounding his mother's death, and Examiner Raynor owed him a favor. Jonah had removed a bullet from the examiner's son's left buttock, the elected official not wanting anyone to know his son had been involved in a gun fight, and as a result had been shot in the ass.

So when Ellie Rybath was found dead in her easy chair on her back porch, Jonah decided to investigate what exactly had killed the woman who had tormented him and his sister most of their lives. He wanted to dig into her flesh and brain, see what made her tick, and ensure that she was in fact human, for he had questioned this numerous times throughout his life. More than that, he wanted to cut her, remove her insides, and leave nothing but an empty shell. This is what she deserved, for she had been evil, and Jonah refused to let her go to the afterlife intact.

It was no accident that Jonah was unstable. When they were kids, his mother would often lock him and his sister, Clara, in the closet for hours on end, only letting them out when she was ready to beat them, or make them perform chores. Ellie Rybath's history was totally unknown to her children—including who their father was—and she would disappear regularly, leaving Clara and Jonah in the care of Ms. Whilly, a huge woman that treated them better than their mother, but still less than human. This prolonged torture unhinged Jonah's mind at an early age, and his insanity only seemed to grow as he got older.

Jonah turned down a narrow alley, descended a series of steps, and passed through several doors, finally coming to a locked one. He knocked on the metal door as hard as he could, and gentle booms echoed through the hallway. Examiner Raynor greeted Jonah and led him down a long hallway to the morgue, were several bodies lay atop gurneys all about the large room. It reeked of embalming fluids and antiseptic, and Jonah felt the urge to cover his nose, but knew Raynor was watching him, so instead he breathed gently through his mouth.

"She's over here," said Raynor, and seeing Jonah's discomfort, he added, "I'll move her into room three so you a have a little privacy, and then I'm heading out. Leave your notes so I can write up the final report." Jonah nodded as he stared down at a cart holding various instruments: a stainless steel bone saw, skull chisel, rib cutter, scalpel, large scissors, and other silver tools he didn't recognize rested atop white linen.

Jonah searched the large room with his eyes as he followed Examiner Raynor and his dead mother to room three, but he saw nothing out of the ordinary. The concrete walls were painted white, and there were several sinks and tables, all made of stainless steel. Jonah carried the tools he had borrowed from the cart, and when the body had been placed beneath the large light in room three, Jonah laid out the instruments as Raynor stripped off his gloves. "Don't forget to shut off all the lights and lock everything down." Jonah nodded again, his eyes locked on his mother, a wicked grin spreading across his pale face.

Raynor saw the insanity in Jonah's eyes, and he wondered what Ellie Rybath had done to deserve the hatred her son felt for her. "OK, then," said Raynor, as he slipped away.

Jonah pulled off the sheet that covered his mother, and saw that someone had already taken off her clothes and cleaned her. Her dark eyes stared up at him with contempt as he began his visual inspection, first checking her feet and toes, then moving up to her vagina, where he took a swab sample. Then he closed her eyes, and flipped her over, examining the back of her head and moving downward.

He had seen his mother naked when he was a boy, and the unfortunate incident involving an unlocked bathroom door had tormented him his entire life, but in death the fear had faded. Then he noticed the small tattoo on her right thigh. It was skull, with two knives running through it. He had never seen the symbol before, and hadn't known his mother had body art. He carefully drew the symbol on his private notepad, then continued his inspection.

Once completed, he flipped her over onto her back again, opened her eyes with the tips of his fingers, and then began cutting her skin away with the oversized scalpel. He smiled as he worked, but was somewhat disappointed that very little blood spilt from the wounds he created. Frustrated, he lifted the rib cutter and began sheering his mother's breast plate and ribs until her torso was open and her organs exposed. After examining her chest cavity, he began ripping the organs from her chest, pulling on them so violently that broken blood vessels and other small pieces of her anatomy flew about the table and onto the floor.

Jonah's eyes glowed with delight at the sight of her empty chest, and he moved on to her eyes, pulling each free with a *pop* and examining them under the harsh overhead light. Then he tossed each eye into a silver bucket where he had collected the rest of the organs. Moving down what remained of his mother's body, he sliced open her uterus with the scalpel, peeling it open like an orange.

What he saw therein made him pause in his insanity.

The birthing of a child leaves a very clear scar within the women's uterus. Other smaller scars can often be seen, which can represent miscarriages, abortions, or other issues. But babies brought to full term leave clear marks of their passing, and as Jonah stared into his mother's uterus in disbelief, he saw three clearly defined scars, though he and his sister had been his mother's only children.

Jonah stood up straight, rubbing his eyes. His mother had given birth to a third child. Jonah tossed the scalpel across the room. It hit the wall with a *clang*, and fell to the floor. Even from beyond the grave, his mother was tormenting him, and this latest surprise gave rise to an anger within him that he could not squelch. Picking up the skull chisel, Jonah brought it down hard on his mother's head, splitting it open, fluid and decaying brain oozing out onto the table. Jonah laughed in his frenzy. He would find this bastard child. He would find it, and kill it.

***

It didn't take Jonah long to discover what his long lost sibling's name was. The city records clearly showed that on the night of June 19th, 1913, Ellie Rybath had given birth to fraternal twins, Jonah and Julius. After that initial break, Jonah had searched for five years, finding no one by the name of Julius Rybath, and Jonah was forced to deal with the fact that his brother most likely had a different name, wasn't in or around Baltimore, or was dead.

With no description of his brother, Jonah simply asked people around town if they had seen a man who looked like him, and told them that the man was his lost brother who he was searching for. A true enough story that Jonah was able to keep his mental justification for hunting the man, as he continued the search for Julius as though the man held some secret Jonah had been looking for his entire life, and his haunted search became his daily obsession.

The knowledge that he was second fiddle only served to stoke his insanity, and drive him harder. Clearly his bitch of a mother coveted Julius over him, and had separated them at birth. Why had she done this? Where had his brother lived his life? The search for Julius was no longer about his dead mother, and desecrating her body and soul. Now his insanity had turned to Julius, his new motive so clear hatred and anger rose in him like a smothering tide, and even the small bit of reason he had used to conduct his life had been discarded. Hatred. Envy. Madness. These were the things that drove him.

It had been simple chance that ultimately led Jonah to his brother. He had traveled all over Baltimore, attending various events, eating and drinking at a different establishment every night, asking questions. He even had a drawing done that showed a man a bit older than himself, with slightly longer hair, that he showed around as though he were searching for a suspect, and he was a cop. This act led him to a private table with Ms. Leigh Valdmore, a dancer at an exotic bar down on the pier. She had seen a man that matched the picture—had seen him many times. He was a regular at her place, and as Jonah gave the woman a small stack of bills and asked her to forget she'd ever met him, her eyes had grown wide. She reached out to hug him, but Jonah had already gone.

The Tender Trap was as big of a shithole on the inside as it was on the outside. Women of dubious beauty gyrated on bar tops, and barmaids ran about in dresses that amounted to little more than bikinis. Jonah had purchased clothing from a local church's second-hand shop, and so didn't look all that out of place amongst the sailors, dock hands, steel workers, and business men who crowded around the prettiest girls like wolves around Red Riding Hood, throwing money like they were tossing fish at seals.

When his brother came in, Jonah ducked into a booth, hiding behind the high-back seat, peering around its edge. Now having seen the man, Jonah had no doubts he was his brother, as the resemblance was unmistakable. He moved with the same ease, his dark hair and pale skin the same as Jonah's. Julius wasted little time, and before he even ordered a drink three women were pressing themselves against him, kissing him, and coaxing money from his pockets.

Jonah slipped from The Tender Trap and hid in the shadows of an abandoned warehouse across the street, where he had a perfect view of the entrance. When his brother came out, Jonah followed him as he made his way across Baltimore before disappearing down a narrow alley between two old stone buildings. Hiding in the shadows, Jonah approached the end of the alley and saw his brother pass through a door. When he came to the door he pulled on it, but it was locked, a large keyhole visible below the doorknob.

Jonah turned to leave, but saw a small symbol etched into the building's stone façade. It was a skull with two knives passing through it. The sight of the symbol stopped Jonah dead, and he stared at the etching as though it were a map to Solomon's Mines. Then he noticed the writing beneath the symbol, which was faded and barely visible. Jonah brushed at the stone with his hand, clearing away years of dirt and grime. Beneath the symbol, the words "The Order of Poe" could be seen.

Perplexed, Jonah slowly backed out of the alley, his mind reeling. The Order of Poe was rumored to be comprised of people who practiced dark religion, including animal sacrifices and other abominations. The Poe Society, which was considered the legitimate group of those who looked to keep Edgar Allan Poe's memory and writings alive, and preserve his history, had attempted many times to get the police to shut down The Order of Poe, but they could never find any evidence of wrongdoing, or any witnesses willing to testify to anything illegal.

After midnight, people began exiting the alley, one by one, all wrapped in dark cloaks, their faces hidden even though there was no one to see them. Julius was able to give Jonah the slip in this way, as all the figures looked the same as they left the gathering and spread out across the city.

The next night at the Tender Trap, his brother showed up right on time, but on this particular night he closed the place. It was 3:45 a.m., January 19th, 1955, and as Jonah followed his brother, he could tell he wasn't going to The Order of Poe on this night. Julius made a right on W. Baltimore Street, and then paused as he was met by a man who handed him a satchel. Jonah watched as his brother accepted the package from the man, and continued on his way.

When he reached Greene Street, Julius looked around to see if anyone was following him, then opened the shoulder bag and took out three red roses, a white scarf, a wide-brimmed hat, and a bottle. Abandoning the bag on the sidewalk, Julius slipped the scarf around his neck, dropped the hat on his head, and made his way down Greene Street toward a fence that surrounded a graveyard. Along the exterior of the fence, all along the sidewalk, benches waited for weary pedestrians, and as Julius came to one, he stepped up onto it, and deftly vaulted over the fence.

The moon glaring down at him, Jonah crept across the silent street and peered through the fence into a cemetery beyond, and it was then that

Jonah realized where he was: Westminster Presbyterian Church. Jonah watched as Julius took a pull of brandy from the ornate cognac bottle, lifted the bottle to the heavens, and then downed its contents. Then he left the three roses and the bottle next to a gravestone, and disappeared into the foliage. Jonah pulled free his flashlight and shone it on the headstone where Julius had placed his items, but he still couldn't read it, so he took out his miniature spyglass and trained it on the gravestone. It read: Quoth the Raven, Nevermore. Original Burial Place. Edgar Allan Poe.

***

After a little research, Jonah learned that what he had seen wasn't the first time a mysterious stranger had left gifts on Poe's grave for his birthday. It had started on the 100th anniversary of his birth, in 1949, the year Jonah's mother had died, and had continued every year since. Jonah concluded that the paying of respects to the man that was the center of their order was in some way part of their ceremonies, but he would find out for sure tonight.

Jonah was certain the Order of Poe would have a meeting the day after Poe's birthday since they had most likely skipped meeting on his birthday to avoid drawing attention to the organization, and they didn't disappoint. People streamed into the alley from every direction, and it hadn't taken much for Jonah to blend into a group as they entered the alleyway, everyone dressed as he was in black cloaks. No one noticed him as they passed through the alley and into the large stone building. On the outside it looked like an old church, but on the inside Jonah could see that it had once been a bank or financial institution of some kind, because there were still teller windows in the rear of the large open space, and abandoned offices around the edge. At midnight, the doors were locked and a man in red appeared to take a head count.

In the center of the room, pinned to a table by its paws, was a mid-sized dog which had been shaved of all its hair. The beast whimpered faintly, all four paws leaking blood from the thick nails that had been hammered through its paws into the wood table. There was no circle of people, as one would expect, but rather folding chairs were lined up in ordered ranks creating a hexagon, the petrified dog at its center.

When the hall was almost full, Jonah began searching for his brother, and on this night he was easy to find. He was the only one with his hood down, face exposed, and he stood on an altar overlooking the crowd, his dark eyes pausing every few seconds to look on one of his followers. Then, without warning, his brother lifted a large knife from beneath his cloak, and plunged it into the whimpering animal. It howled in pain, and then fell silent.

"Another year we pray. Another year we await the rebirth. As you all saw in the papers this morning, I was successful in my task." Julius bowed his head, and Jonah used that moment to make his move. He was through the crowd, onto the altar, and was holding a gun to his brother's head before anyone in the room knew what was happening.

"Anyone moves and he's dead," said Jonah, smiling at the crowd.

Seeing the resemblance between them, Julius hissed, "You must be Jonah. We finally meet."

This stunned Jonah, and he threw his brother to the ground, putting his foot on his chest and the gun to his head. "You knew of me?"

"Of course. Mother knew you were too weak to be here. That's why I was chosen to be head of the order. She saw you as nothing more than a damaged animal."

Jonah stared at his brother, anger swelling within him. He said, "Damaged?"

"Oh, Jonah. You don't know anything, do you? Clara knew this. Did she never tell you? Mother didn't know she was having twins, and when you emerged several minutes after me, she knew it was a curse. Had it not been for the doctor and nurse, she would have killed you right there and ended the charade. As it was, I lived among the order, learning their ways, and preparing to lead. You, well…"

Pop!

Jonah had heard all he needed to. Julius' body lay limp on the altar, blood spreading out around his head. Jonah felt the eyes on him then, the Order of Poe not knowing what to do next. "People," yelled Jonah, knowing for the first time in his life what he must do with 100% surety. He pulled free a magnificent lie, and one that would cement his future in ways he had never thought possible.

"I am the true priest here. My brother was but a copy. I will lead you now." One by one, the Order of Poe knelt before Jonah, his brother's fallen body lying on the altar before him. If there was an afterlife, Jonah hoped his mother watched him from it now. He had proven her wrong yet again. He was the worthy one, the strong one, and he would continue the Order of Poe's traditions and take on his brother's duties. As everyone in the hall began to moan and chant his name, Jonah felt whole for the first time in his life.

***

The Huffington Post
January 19th, 2010

Edgar Allan Poe's Mysterious Visitor Doesn't Show This Year

BALTIMORE — It is what Edgar Allan Poe might have called "a mystery all insoluble." Every year for the past six decades, a shadowy visitor would leave roses and a half-empty bottle of cognac on Poe's grave on the anniversary of the writer's birth. This year, no one showed.

Did the mysterious "Poe toaster" meet his own mortal end? Did some kind of ghastly misfortune befall him? Will he be heard from nevermore?

"I'm confused, befuddled," said Jeff Jerome, curator of the Poe House and Museum. "I don't know what's going on."

The visitor's absence this year only deepens the mystery over his identity.

AUNTIE GRAVE
Jessica McHugh

The briar road is long and its tortures unending. There, Auntie Grave plays her bone piccolo, beckoning those who dare to interrupt the balance created by her sister, Lady Life, and her brother, Lord Death. We are their children and must obey their laws. But Auntie Grave lives barren, playing her sad song in the hopes that the lawbreakers will fill her belly. That we will die in her arms and be reborn as living corpses in her briar patches.

Marla switched off the flashlight, and her glowing grimace disappeared. Her brother Gary cocked his head, his eyebrows raised.

"Then what happened?" he asked.

"What do you mean?"

"That wasn't a scary story. All you did was describe this Auntie Grave person."

"She's not a person."

"You still didn't finish it. How does someone interrupt life and death? Where is this road? Has anyone ever seen it?" His sister shrugged. "You're not a very good storyteller. You know that, right?"

"You said you wanted to hear something scary."

"I'm still waiting for the scary part. Bloody Mary is scarier than that shit."

Marla threw the flashlight, but Gary caught it with a chuckle, hurling it back before she could deflect it with her pillow.

"Ow, stop!" she whined.

Marla coughed repeatedly, and Gary rolled his eyes.

"Come on, do your thing," he groaned over her coughing fit.

She took a few puffs from her inhaler and caught her breath. Even then, it was strained, and her face drooped, pale and clammy.

THE GRAVEYARD EDITION

The closet door opened, and Mrs. Hammond's scowl poked inside.

"What are you two doing in here?"

"Telling scary stories—well, I was," Gary said. "Marla's just describing dumb stuff."

"It's not dumb. It's real," she insisted.

"Maybe it's time for you two to get to bed. You have a big day tomorrow." She crouched beside Marla and bopped her on the nose. "Especially you, birthday girl."

"What's so big about it? It's just stupid church," Gary grumbled.

"Gary…"

"I know, I know. It's not stupid. Birthdays and saving our souls and stuff. I just don't understand why we have to go back after all this time. We were fine without it. I'd rather sleep late and play video games than sit on a stinky bench for three hours."

"I never thought it was stinky," Marla said.

"Why else do you think it's called a peee-ewww?" he laughed. "Maybe you couldn't smell it because you stink so bad."

"Shut up!"

She coughed again. Mrs. Hammond popped an inhaler into Marla's mouth and squeezed, the medication filling her lungs.

"Lemme take a puff," Gary said.

"No, your sister needs it all," she replied. "Now, it's time for both of you to come out of there and go to bed. I want you well-rested for tomorrow."

She tousled her daughter's hair, and Marla looked up at her with smile.

"I'm glad to be going to church, Mommy."

"Suck up," Gary mumbled.

"I'm not kidding—both of you to bed."

"Just one more story?" Marla asked. "Please, Mom, it'll be short."

"And boring. Marley can't tell a scary story for shi—" He glanced up at his mother's stiff expression. "—shucks."

"Okay, one more story, then it's straight to bed."

"Yeah, yeah." Once their mother had closed the door, Gary crinkled his nose and said, "Okay, dummy, do your worst."

Marla smirked, positioning the flashlight under her chin. When she flicked it on, Gary was surprised to feel his skin prickle. He rubbed the goosebumps away and leaned against a stack of board games with a forced yawn. Marla took a puff from her inhaler and began.

"Once upon a time, there was a boy who was mean to his little sister."

"Oh jeez. Was his name Gary?" he groaned, shutting his eyes.

"The day his sister was born, he went to his parents and said, 'The new baby screams too much. I don't like her. I'm going to kill her.' His parents were obviously upset, but they didn't think he'd actually do anything. They were wrong."

Gary opened his eyes and sat up straight.

"On the twelfth day after their daughter's birth, the parents realized the baby hadn't cried in hours. In her room, they discovered the crib empty and the closet door ajar. There, covered with a pillow, they found their infant daughter—dead. Their son swore up and down he didn't do it, but his parents didn't believe him. I mean, would you?"

Gary shrugged. "Go on."

"After the baby was buried, they took the boy to a doctor—one that puts you into a trance."

"A hypnotist."

"Right. The hypnotist put him in a trance to get the truth. The boy eventually admitted to killing his baby sister by smothering her with a pillow. But something else happened, too. The boy…changed."

"Changed how?" Gary asked, leaning forward.

"His voice, his face, even his body—he changed into an old woman, right in front of them. His hair fell out, his bones shrank, and his skin sagged. When he spoke, his teeth cracked and slipped out of his gums. His tongue curled up in the back of his throat, dry and gray as an old fish, but his words came out clear as a bell.

"He said, 'Wicked children are a waste, unholy holes in time and space. If a sweet one's life you wish to save, call on me, your Auntie Grave.'"

"Oh God, not this Auntie Grave stuff again."

"You wanted the full story, didn't you?"

"I guess."

"So be quiet and let me finish." She sucked on her inhaler and cleared her throat.

"'What do you want?' the father asked his son.

"'Unearth the goodly flesh and bone, and wait for Auntie to atone. The days you had, you'll have in years—with a lifelong chance to dry your tears. Your choices will the long road pave, to follow the song of Auntie Grave.'

"The old woman collapsed, and the boy's original features returned. His parents didn't know what to do. Nothing the woman said had changed anything. Their baby was still dead, and their son had still killed her."

The closet door opened. "That's long enough," Mrs. Hammond chirped.

"Come on, Mom, she was just getting to the good part," Gary whimpered.

"It's okay," Marla said, standing. "The good part can wait till tomorrow."

"But I want to know what happens."

"Not scared, are you?" she asked.

Gary scoffed. "No, just curious."

"You'll still be curious tomorrow," their mother said. "Out, now, and to bed."

Gary grumbled, pushing past Marla to exit the closet first.

"It was a stupid story anyway," he said. "Like stupid church and your stupid birthday. Next time, come up with something scary, or I'm done wasting my time with you."

He tromped into his bedroom, slamming the door behind him. Nothing could frighten him, especially not an eleven year old with asthma. But alone in his room, the goosebumps came again. Even with the lights on the place had never seemed so dark.

"Marley, what did you say to him?" Mrs. Hammond asked. Marla smiled before the inhaler filled her lungs. "Uh huh, off to bed. Big day tomorrow."

"The biggest, Mommy."

While her mother tucked her into bed, Gary heard her through the wall, telling Marla how much she loved her. He didn't care. He was too old for that baby stuff anyway. But as Gary flipped off his light, climbed into his creaking bed, and pulled the sheets to his chin, he found himself longing for baby stuff.

Based the monsters he spotted in the dark, Gary assumed he'd fallen asleep. They were massive, with bulging muscles that split their skin and spurted oily blood. He was used to those devils whispering from midnight shadows, so they were easily rationalized away. But amidst the bulging blackness appeared a shadow Gary didn't recognize.

Thinner and grayer, the new wisp danced unafraid between the monstrous hordes. Their snarling died to low rumbles—bass to a new and eerie tune piercing the night. As the gray ghost floated across Gary's walls, the song grew shriller, so abrasive that he had to cover his ears. The shadow moved to his closet door, where it reached out, its slender fingers beckoning the boy forward.

Gary told himself he wasn't afraid. He would open the closet, scream for the ghost to shut up, and slam the door closed, smashing the gray bitch to smithereens. Growling in hubris, he leapt from his bed and yelled "Ha!" as he pulled open the closet door.

There were no monsters or shadows inside. There were also no clothes, no shoes, or roller skates that had bored him after two days. There was only a gray road, stretching on for eternity. Lined with immense briar hedges, the road called him, the music more tempting in a distant calm.

With a bold step forward, he spotted fluttering clothes in the briars. Hair, too. And skin. Eyes, staring dead. Frowning faces ripped into grins.

From the bottom to the top, people were tangled in the hedges, squirming for freedom. The briars slashed them deeper, but even the occasional sever didn't slow their wriggling.

Gary backpedaled, smacking his head against the closed closet. He twisted the knob and kicked the door, but it wouldn't budge. Turning to the road in panic, Gary faced two terrifying figures. He wasn't sure which scared him more: the distant woman playing a bone piccolo, or the baby lying motionless in the road, a pillow covering its face.

"Wicked child, wicked child," the woman sang, her ulnar instrument wailing.

Gary covered his ears, but he heard the voice clearer. He crumpled to his knees, sobbing. Trapped inside his head, the music sounded more and more like a bawling baby. In desperation, he crawled to the infant and lifted the pillow.

He quaked at the baby's swollen, purple face, its mouth a toothless cavern frozen in an eternal shriek. The top of its skull was sunken and covered with russet scales, and though its belly was distended, its limbs were curled inward, brittle and flaking gray. He tried to cover the horrific infant, but the pillow was ripped from his hands by an unseen force.

The baby giggled, and its eyes snapped open. Its body convulsed as a brown hash smelling of earth and rotten meat filled its mouth, spraying clods of slimy dirt at Gary's face. He scrambled to the closet, beating the door and screaming Marla's name.

The hand on his shoulder turned him around to face the grisly old woman. There were barely enough panels of skin stretched over her skull to consider it a face. Thin ropes of silver hair hung in front, blowing across her mouth as she gnawed on soggy chunks of soil. She didn't speak, but when she latched onto his arm, Gary knew her name was "Auntie Grave."

***

"Jeez, Gary, turn off your alarm!" Marla said, flicking his nose

He sprang up, gasping for air, his pillow clutched to his chest. His alarm screamed repetitive beeps until he silenced it with a smack.

Marla poked his sheets, her lip curled. "Did you wet the bed?"

"No, I was hot, that's all," Gary scoffed.

"Wait—did you have a nightmare? From my boring story?"

"No way! I told you, I was hot."

"Whatever," she snickered. "You better hurry up, or we're going to be late for church."

"Big deal."

"It is a big deal. It's my birthday, remember?"

"Like I could ever forget with you reminding me every second," he grumbled. "Oh, and just to get the disappointment out of the way now, I don't have anything for you."

"Huh?"

"I didn't buy you a present."

Gary braced himself for a tantrum, but Marla smiled. "That's okay. I wasn't expecting you to buy me anything," she said. "But you could wish me happy birthday."

He threw his pillow at her, covering himself with the sweaty sheets as he muttered, "Get out."

The Hammonds were late leaving the house. Gary claimed he couldn't find his church shoes, but he'd actually spent the time investigating his closet to make sure what he'd seen had been a dream. Satisfied, he settled into the car to play Mario on his Nintendo DS. He jumped on turtles and collected coins all the way to First Presbyterian, even as his father parked the car. He paid no attention as his parents led him and Marla through the empty parking lot, around the church, or to the cemetery behind it. It wasn't until he lost his last life that he looked up, nearly crashing into a headstone.

"What are we doing here?" Gary asked.

Marla crept up on him, wriggling her fingers in his face as she moaned, "Waiting for Auntie Grave." She laughed and smacked her brother on the shoulder.

"That's not funny."

"You should've seen your face. You were so scared!"

"No, I wasn't!"

"Admit it, you were scared."

"Like a baby story would ever scare me. 'Auntie Grave?' That's so lame."

"It's not a baby story," Marla said. "Mom and Dad told it to me."

"Bull."

"It's true, Gary," Mr. Hammond said, touching his son's shoulder. "We told it to her when she was five."

"Whatever. It's still not scary."

"Good, that will make this easier," Mrs. Hammond said.

Marla sat down on a headstone, coughing. Her mother handed an inhaler to her daughter, but it didn't help. Shaking it, she realized it was empty.

"I'll do it this time," her father said, kneeling on the gravesite. He unscrewed the canister and dug it through the soil. Handing the inhaler back to his daughter, she squeezed it into her mouth. Taking a deep breath, the soil filled her grateful lungs.

"What the—" Gary squeaked.

"It's the only way I can breathe," Marla said. "No thanks to you." She cuddled against her mother, her father kissing her forehead. "How much longer?" she asked them.

Mrs. Hammond looked at her watch. "In two minutes, you'll be exactly twelve years old."

"To match the number of days you were alive," her father added.

Shivers filled Gary's belly. "What are you guys talking about?" he asked.

"We made our choice, son. This road was paved long ago with your wickedness—when you killed your sister."

"No, that's not possible," he panted. "I don't remember that."

"But we do," his mother said. "Your father and I have had to live with what you did, pretending to love you, counting the years until we could make a permanent exchange."

"Please don't do this. I'll be good. I'll be—"

Gary's breath thinned, and his words disappeared in a strangled squeal. Mr. Hammond's watch beeped, and Marla dropped her inhaler to the ground.

When a playful piccolo called him from the distance, Gary sank to his sister's grave, unable to breathe.

A DIARY OF MADNESS
Georgina Morales

Mother, night has fallen upon me. I am sick and cold and frightened. Outside my refuge, a monster bides its time, prolonging my suffering, letting my mind succumb to lunacy before it grabs hold of my neck once more. I don't think I'll live to see the morrow, and I fear I am too late to get to your bedside. Still, I hold on dear to your memory, like the source of strength you always were. As I relate my unbelievable tale, forgive my distractions; you cannot blame your son for fearing the terror that paces outside his abode.

The fever has increased and noises effervesce in the forest, but not of the natural, merry kind. Animals cry, the wind howls, and disembodied moans warn me of what awaits me outside. She's closing in, the foreboding presence I first encountered close to that cursed river. Can she not be real? Is she a vision? A vision from hell that's come for me? Yet, the coldness in my skin as she brushes past me feels too real. I must not sleep for my soul, might get lost in this tragic forest, trapped forever in the realm of the beast. Father almighty, heed thy faithful son for madness is his companion!

To think of my childhood is to think of your lap and your tender, guiding hand. Oh, what a special connection we shared! You alone understood the poet's heart inside of me. You let me fly when all I saw was a golden cage. Oh, Mother, it is to you that I owe the most, and how poorly I repaid. I'm sorry for being an ungrateful son. I wasn't prepared to assume the role you chose for me; I wish I had. As I attempt to unburden my soul, I write my goodbyes to you. Lord, protect this lost soul and allow the feeble hand to leave one last piece of testimony.

This morning the Italian Alps greeted me against a perfect, blue sky. I planned a walk through the woods, six hours of fresh air and charming landscape. I'd spend the night on the outskirts of a town where the train would take me to Genoa, then a boat home. Every detail I took care of with the dedication of a zealot, considering this the closing travel of a youth spent trekking the globe. But I was ready. Ready to go back and fulfill a debt for far too long gone unpaid.

I should have stopped when the first signs of fever began, gone back, got better so I might still have a chance to redeem myself to you. But since no shortage of perils tracked me as I made my way through Europe, I decided experience was on my side. Oh, arrogance, you were quick to charge at my mistake! I see now, Mother, that you were right to treat me like a child, for this experienced traveler not only went on in sickness, but then he got lost.

Why, oh, why did I wander off the path? She beguiled me. The gay laugh of a lady echoed in the woods to my left, so familiar and inviting. Distant memories fluttered within me but none too clear, like the swift swim of a fish avoiding the trapping hand. I needed to know who she was or if we had met before. And I fell prey to the siren's call.

That woman's voice traveled through the forest like a singing bird, and with every note the resolution to find her grew stronger in me. My careful planning was no match for her enchantment. Without a pause or question, I walked down a long-abandoned path, not even considering what I needed for survival under a leafless ceiling. All I could think of was reaching my slippery guide.

The yellow of the sun turned into a deep hue of orange and red, painting in blood the landscape before me. I came in control of my thoughts again, and I wondered where I was. Had I veered too far off my path? Naked vegetation pointed to the sky with boney hands, and I knew, not even garbed in its joyful spring dresses, happiness was never allowed in this forsaken land.

I decided to go no further, to ascertain my bearings and find a way to the lodge I had originally planned. Then the wind carried an unearthly howl, and I shuddered. Beads of sweat ran down my spine. Far among the trees I saw a white glimmering light that filled me with dread. Panic took over. My reason argued the exigency of control, but the heart is tempestuous in its reactions and little can the brain do to subdue it. And although I wanted to run on the opposite direction, my feet moved of their own volition, and I followed the specter still!

I tried to stop myself, tried to turn back, but nothing worked until I lost sight of the glowing, white monster behind a small hill. Sweat covered my forehead and I dared not breathe for fear to call her back. A minute passed. She remained lost, and I was free from her ghostly call! I collapsed to the ground, braking in a jagged laugh of respite. However, I was lost in the forest with no compass, food, or equipment to last until dawn.

If only then I would have remained calm, but I changed directions several times, always trying to find my way back. Finally, I came across a river channel. I followed it for I knew that where there is water, people must be close by. For many hours I saw no sign of hope, and as I resigned to die, from the dense body of trees it appeared before me. Across the river, an old stone cabin stood alone, smoke trickling through its chimney. Relief overwhelmed me. Salvation was in my grasp!

The sky wrapped the scenery in twilight, dressing for night's arrival. I prepared to cross the waterway when, before my eyes, the tranquil stream swelled and ran with treacherous force. Still, my best shot at survival laid on the other side. I repeated the little prayer you taught me so well for times of distress and dived in.

I never imagined a natural spot so synonymous of life brimmed with such evil! The coldness waiting in the turbid waters seeped through my clothes and into my heart. Something writhed at me feet. It moved fast and tangled between my legs, binding them with a force beyond that of any river creature. I grew desperate and fought, reaching for the thing with my hands, and as I touched it, it melted, merging with my soul. The horror! I could feel the monster under my skin, and it howled in victory for I had stepped into its realm.

My heavy limbs made it difficult to move under the murky surface of the water. I looked for something to help me in my fight against the current, and I held to a floating vine. The swollen river carried debris that hurt my feet and legs. They scratched me like fingers searching for my limbs, but it couldn't be. It had to be an illusion caused by fever and fear, I told myself when I reached the ground on the other side. I collapsed on the grass where, too afraid to confront the darkened forest and too tired to move on, I fell asleep. But instead of the resting sleep for the pious souls, the torturous one reserved for the insane besieged me.

In my dream, crimson twilight illuminated the landscape as light rain fell. I walked with weary steps, finding my way through obscured trails littered with rocks. The cold in my bones made me clumsy and I tripped, though the icy temperatures numbed me to the pain. Exhaustion and despair filled me. I asked the heavens to take me, let me rest and die in peace. I wanted to give up. But then I would never see you again. No, I had to keep going. I stood up, determined, but when I looked at my hands, dismay swathed me. They were covered in blood. There was no rain colored by the skylight, it was blood. Every surface was red, the flowers, the grass, the trees. I ran away in terror through an earthen path and dirt became airborne. It fell like snow, in light, delicate flakes that came to rest on top of the unholy scarlet liquid.

What a ghastly spectacle, exceeded only by the sight of a white apparition hovering between the trees. Its ethereal facade was so that I could not distinguish its features or contour, but I realized it remained untouched by the corrupted land. It had a preternatural glow, similar to the one that had led me to the stream. And even though I hadn't confronted it yet, I knew seeing her face would mean my death.

I ran with ever more haste trying to leave the vision behind, but it always kept close. It hid its face behind the trees, letting me glimpse at her eerie robes, closer every time. The unnatural red-tinted woodland whispered condolences. I could not outrun my demise!

As I took one more turn on my path, her grisly sight confronted me. Oh, God, what a dreadful sight! It was you, Mother. It was you! Your toothless mouth in a twisted smile, unable to open, for it was bound by the sad bow with which they silence the dead. Once your skin was rosy and alive, not anymore. Oh, Mother, not anymore. Your flesh was gray and pale. Your once proud stance, a hunched figure secured inside your shroud. How could I fight the assault of insanity when in front of me hung a deranged illusion of the one I adored the most?

"No, horrible creature, be gone! You're not her, you can't be." But the fiend freed its hands from its binds and grabbed hold of my neck. And though it was impossible for it to speak, it did. Oh, it did!

"Benjamin, I gave you freedom in life, but you'll be mine in death." A dreadful laugh cut through the air.

It was the laugh that awoke me. It keeps haunting me, now out of my dreams. Nothing but a nightmare, I tell myself, a concoction of my feverish senses under the traps of exhaustion. Yet, I tremble with the memory of it. It felt so real!

Once awake I gazed at the sky, fighting to gain control over my raw nerves. The moon shone in the firmament and on the ground, a fine coat of snow glittered under its spell, taking me back to the place of my nightmare. My eyes looked for the cabin again. It stood a few yards away, enticing me to come closer, though the signs of occupancy were not evident from this side of the river. Its wooden walls, in an advanced state of decay, would not hold for years to come. The chimney, before exhaling fumes, now half-stood with many bricks missing. And although I did not want to, I advanced toward it. Whatever its state, it would offer a better refuge than the tree branches ever could.

I rushed for I feared the ominous wraith roaming the woods, but every step was a struggle. My legs ached, my head throbbed, and my eyes wanted to jump out of their sockets. I calculated the cabin to be close enough to reach within an hour. Oh, but how deceiving the woods were. For what seemed like hours, I pursued my goal. No matter what different paths I took, the haggard construction kept me at bay. I moved faster. Was my fever playing cruel jokes on me? I prayed the Lord to take pity, yet the cabin remained a few yards away. Although impossible, time appeared to be frozen, and the moon never faltered in its position above my head.

I had to be delirious for it was impossible, I tell you! I traversed dead trees and forgotten paths; I chose one trail over another with the cabin always in my sight. Never did it grow closer! Fever ravaged my innards and soon the diabolical specter was back, moving light behind me, relishing my torture. Like in my dream, it hid its face from me, still I recognized the hunched stance garbed in funeral robes. The murmurs grew clearer and I heard your voice. Was it you, Mother, wailing, lamenting your own death and ready to cause mine?

But I didn't stop in this trial bestowed upon me. I refused to believe the Grim Reaper had taken you, and I walked. I walked until I thought my feet would bleed, until the illness almost robbed me of my sight, until I lost all hope of ever finding the fated cabin. In unbearable pain, I could go no more, and I prepared to atone for my sins, resigned to confront my demon.

It was when defeated I turned the last curve that in front of me stood the doors I so relentlessly had sought. No sooner I entered the place than I recognized it was never a cabin. The final veil had been lifted from my eyes, and I stood where the Fates had always wanted me to be.

The time has come. At my door is the coldness of your presence; or is it the winter breeze blowing through the hollow trees? But that ungodly lament echoing in the woods can be bellowed by no being of this earth. And those sallow feet at my doorway; is that the soil of the exhumed that they bear? My restless mind mocks me, I know; yet, I can't deny what floats in the air, the place where I sit, or the premonition in my skin. God, give me clarity for I must scribble my last words.

I should have returned after Father died, sit next to you and hold your lonely hand. News reached me that you were sick, but I thought there would always be time. Now, inside this eternal home of marble where I hear the unsettling brush of your shroud trickling down the stairs, I know there is naught. Your white splendor reaches me at the base. So shall be the culmination of my story, fittingly forsaking a happy ending for me. And though I tremble, I call upon the memory of our happy years together. My beloved mother, I wish not see your face this way. Let me close my eyes, Lord, and may my soul be with you soon.

***

Benjamin Faraday's story, related as found in his diary lost long ago, tells how his corpse was found in Connecticut, atop his mother's tomb in the family mausoleum. No evidence ever surfaced of how he traveled home. No souvenirs of his life in Europe, nor clothing or valuables were ever shipped. Nothing to speak of his time on earth but a body with reddened marks on the neck and a town talking. Rumors said his mother had collected from beyond the grave, then sightings of a woman in a white, floating shroud began. The old cemetery fell out of use. Maddening cries carried by the wind followed by the echo of a laugh did little to alleviate fear. A legend was born. Reaching far beyond the town's lines, it finds new ears in tourists who, hungry for adventure, enter where the hollow trees stand, never to be seen again.

DIARY OF A DOORMOUSE
Cortney Philip

-For Stitchie Von Poo

Day 1

It's getting cold in the field. The days are shorter, and we wake each morning in nests hardened with frost. Food is scarce. The seeds have stopped dropping from the wheat, so we must dig for what we can. I fear for my sister, who gives all her food to her children.

Day 5

My sister continues to waste away at a rapid pace. Her greedy, black-eyed children look at her as if she's already a corpse. The days are shorter now, with less time for digging. I grow more sluggish as the winter sets in.

Day 8

My sister died sometime in the night. The children gnaw on her bones as I write this. Warm light emanates from the farmhouse at the far edge of our field. I will set out toward it at daybreak and leave these cruel monsters behind.

Day 9

My trek across the field got cut short by the man with his machine, plowing all the dead stalks under. I had to run back almost as far as I came to stay ahead of its teeth. The softer soil it turned up is full of worms and grubs, but for how long? They seek the promise of warmth farther below, as I seek the promise of warmth in the distance. I'm determined to finish my journey to the big house.

Day 10

I have made it as far as the front stoop, which I will rest under tonight. It grows dark, and I have more hope of finding a way in once the sun rises again. I pull loose hay and dead leaves around me, and pray my belly full of grubs will heat me in my nest until daybreak.

Day 11

In these lean times, it was no challenge to squeeze myself in through a cracked window. My bones feel light as air! Now, to find a secret place in this house to dwell.

Day 14

I have taken up residence in a neat hole in the wall of the great room where the human family spends most of their leisure time. I can observe their comings and goings throughout the day, though they cannot see me. The entrance to my hole is partially obscured by a rack of fireplace tools, which they use to turn the logs and poke at the embers of the constant fire. I do not remember ever having felt such warmth in all my life!

Day 16

Every time I attempt to leave my hole to forage for food, a dark shadow crosses over my path and chases me back inside. I fear this beast guards me day and night. My belly has been empty for days, and I long for a meal of turned-up worms in the field. Even my claws have grown thin and brittle. I chew the ragged ends off slowly to savor the only meal I can find.

Day 17

The shadow still falls when I poke my head out to peer around. I am slowly going crazy cooped up in here with nothing but my thoughts for food. Three times now I have stirred from a reverie to discover I am pulling my own fur out in clumps. Unfortunately, I have discovered that hair is both unpalatable and indigestible. What would happen if I kept going, despite the shadow? Would the creature manifest itself as something more solid? I must make a plan and execute it forthwith.

Day 20

Dear reader, please excuse my long silence. My plan was only half successful. As I came out of my hole, the shadow fell as expected. I ran as fast as my weakened legs would carry me, and I made it into the pantry where I found a hunk of bread that had fallen to the floor. I bit into this piece of sweet, stale salvation as the shadow caught up to me, hissing and spitting with rage. I could have sworn it was feline in nature, though the worst kind of feral, mangy cat that normally only skulks around behind chicken coops in the early morning, scavenging for the foxes' leftovers. I managed to drag the bread as I ran back to my hole, which was no small feat due to the wounds I received. If I exercise discipline and only eat small nibbles each day, I should have enough to sustain me through my recovery.

Day 23

The warmth of the fire that I so appreciated after the cold nights in the field has become unbearable as I swelter, alone and hungry. Since I cannot leave to relieve myself, my hole is dank with the smell of my own feces. My wounds are not healing as quickly as I had hoped and fester in this stagnant air. The worst part is that I have run out of bread and know I must venture out again soon if I am to survive at all.

Day 24

I have often observed the woman of the house taking an urn from the mantle of my fireplace and holding it in her lap for several minutes before putting it up again and going on about her chores. Today, she performed this ritual with a slight variation. This time, she rubbed the urn and murmured "Patches, Patches" before returning it to its spot. What does it mean, and what is this "Patches" she is attempting to stroke from the container?

Day 25

I discovered I am still too weak to forage, though I have allowed myself to convalesce for too long. My muscles have atrophied, and my wounds continue to ooze. My shrunken stomach burns, and I imagine my unused bile slowly eating away at my insides. I ran back toward the pantry to perhaps find more bread, and the shadow nearly consumed me in its snarling whirlwind. One of my hind legs drags a bit now as the result of my new wounds.

Day 27

Half-dead in my hole last night, my bowels constricted something fierce. Though I did not at first understand the cause of my duress and after I had writhed in agony for several hours, two young gradually heaved out of me. One was already dead, and the other looked like she would be soon to follow. I ate my thin placenta—nourishment!—and pushed the children from my nest. It would have been smart to eat them, too, but I had scarcely the heart to do so. As soon as they crossed over my modest threshold, the black shadow descended and carried them away.

Day 28

Today I watched as the woman of the house reprimanded the urn she takes from the mantle. As she held the container in her arms and rocked, she asked it why the room was in such disarray. "The newspaper has been scattered across the floor, and it stinks like wet cat in here," she said as she stroked. "Oh, Patches," she said, "how I've missed you."

Day 29

Fear of dying bereft in my dank and fetid cell drove me again to the pantry in search of food. Nothing crossed my path nor interfered with my mission, and I was permitted to make several trips back and forth to carry provisions to my home. It is indeed possible to eke out an existence in this place, and surely I cannot be the only one who has come here seeking refuge from the winter and survived. I know now what I must do to appease the fanged shadow, and I contemplate how I will become pregnant with my next brood.

THE GRAVEYARD EDITION

AND ALL THE TRIMMINGS
Jennifer A. Smith

All of the Christmas things are in the attic. The lights, the ornaments, boxes, everything you can imagine. Everything that I can imagine anyway... The attic scares me, it always had. I had grown up in the house and had feared the attic every day and especially every night. At the age of 13, I was given the bedroom in the attic; well it was attached to the attic. It was supposed to be a delicious rite of passage to have the attic room; it was almost like my own apartment. I would have felt that way if it weren't for the noises and the voices and the god knows what, that populated the attic proper.

The only security I had to keep those creatures at bay was a little hook and eye latch on the doorway that led to the storage area. I supplemented that bit of security with piles of books that I placed in front of the door. I also had a list of phrases that I would recite each night to keep the creatures safely behind the door, and the last bit of protection was to sleep with a pillow over my head...

Each evening, as darkness came rushing in my windows, things started happening. The low level whispering I heard during the daylight turned into shouts and screams. And the scraping, something scraped the floor boards as it moved. I lived in complete fear, staying away from the upstairs until it was noticed that I was still up. Then I would be rousted out of whatever hiding place I had found and ordered up to my room to sleep.

Tonight was the night we trimmed the tree. My mother and I had walked three blocks to the Christmas tree lot and had carried it home. I was, as always, dreadfully embarrassed by this, but my mom said we looked like a Christmas card. After arriving home, we placed the tree in its stand and stood back to admire our work. Then my mother said the dreaded words, "Jenny, run up to the attic and bring down the Christmas ornaments. Hurry now, I want it to be ready when your father gets home."

I didn't want to go up there but I couldn't let anyone else see how I had barricaded the doorway, so there was no other choice. It was still daylight but I didn't want to look at whatever was behind the door. I knew it would be the death of any sort of peace of mind I had ever had.

I climbed the steps, all thirteen of them. I walked to the attic door and hesitated, almost sobbing with fear. I moved the books, one by one, hoping that the ritual would save me. But as I moved the books out of the way, I began to hear renewed activities beyond the door. There were screams, and creaks, and spurts of laughter. With the books out of the way, I unlatched the lock and slowly opened the door. I was so nervous by now that the sight of nothing much in front of me rattled me even more. I stepped into the cold, foul smelling area, and rushed into the far corner where the Christmas stuff was always stored. I grabbed three boxes, dropped one, and all of the ornaments and old tinsel scattered on the dusty, scary attic floor. I left the stuff where it was and rushed out into my room, slamming and locking the door behind me. I couldn't possibly go back in to get the ornaments that had fallen; surely the two boxes I retrieved would be enough for now.

I brought the two boxes down to the living room. My mom asked "Is that all you could find? I'm pretty sure that there are a few more boxes up there."

"Mom, I couldn't carry it all, maybe I could get the rest tomorrow," I stammered. She shrugged her shoulders in apparent irritation and she opened the boxes and started to trim the tree. So, I was safe for now, at least until I had to go up to bed.

After staying up as long as I could get away with, I quietly went up to bed. I quickly restacked the books in front of the door and recited my litany of protective verses. But, even as I jumped into the bed and placed the pillow and blanket over me, I could feel them in the attic, growling and plotting. They knew I would have to go in there and pick up the spilled Christmas things and they were planning the horrible deeds they would commit once I was in their realm.

I couldn't fall asleep, the pillow on my face made me feel claustrophobic, and the blanket made me feel hot. I felt like a sitting duck, all I was doing by covering my ears was to make it easier for them to get to me. But there was no choice at all. Listening to the noises would kill me, I would die from fear. I might anyway as I listened to my heartbeat, it seemed to get louder and louder, the more I held the pillow over my head.

And then I heard it. I heard the unmistakable sound of my books being pushed slowly away by the opening of the attic door. I heard some books fall over and then a scratching sound, like a lobster claw being dragged across the floor. Something sharp was clattering over my floor. I opened my eyes just a slit and saw a strange jagged shadow where there should be nothing.

My mouth went dry and I felt sick. Should I play dead or attack? I decided to do nothing and hope that it went away. After all, how could I fight a monster? I quickly lost the ability to breathe naturally and I knew that there was no choice anymore. I had to confront the shadows and finally find out who they were and what they wanted from me. Maybe they had come to visit me in the Christmas spirit. Perhaps they were good monsters…

The teddy bear, he was a teddy bear, looked so familiar. I had gotten him for Christmas about 5 years ago and had quickly tired of him. He had been relegated to the attic with all of the other toys that I didn't play with anymore.

The incredibly tall Raggedy Ann doll had apparently grown up over the last several years. Her clothing was painfully tight and short. Her blue eyes were dusty and cruel; she fixed them upon me with loathing and I quailed at the sight of her hatred.

Then there was the clown. He was grinning maliciously. He was a clown born to be swatted. His talent was that he didn't ever fall down. But I wouldn't dare to strike him now, he had definitely changed. They all had. They were after revenge.

The teddy was the first to speak. He started out growling and slowly changed over to words. His voice was thick with anger and injustice. "You, you, were afraid of the attic. You knew the evil that dwelled there and yet you put us in boxes and locked us in. We've been suffering for years, tormented by the devils that thrive there in the dark and damp. We screamed and cried for your help. You did nothing. We have been changed by our years of torment. The hatred we felt for you was all that kept us alive. It's your turn now" he said.

The others nodded their heads and made menacing noises at me. They weren't as eloquent as the Teddy but their intent was obvious. They were going to lock me in the attic now. Raggedy Ann grabbed the sleeve of my nightgown, the clown's dangling claws dug into my arm and they dragged me across the rug, over the linoleum, and finally into the attic. They pushed me into a far corner; stuffed old papers in my mouth, and the clown ripped open my throat. I became quiet, not quite dead and certainly not alive. But I could hear the creaking and moaning of the other creatures, the ones that had been there forever. Something was crawling down my throat, and I closed my eyes again and tried not to notice.

THE BALLAD OF DRUNKEN JACK
K.R. Smith

Priscilla was no beauty,
And suitors were but few,
Though all that knew her and her heart
Swore her words were true.

She dreamed of handsome gentlemen
To take her far away,
Yet as her years and youth did pass
Those dreams began to fade

Till only one man came to call,
A man who had a knack
Of flirting with the local girls,
Known as Drunken Jack,

And wishing not to be alone,
Would sneak off from her chores
To meet him at the tavern,
Waiting by the door.

From there they walked into the hills
Where romance took its course
Until her love began to show
With child whose fate was cursed.

For when she told Jack of her plight,
Pleading as she cried,
Said if she told anyone
He'd say that she had lied.

Despite his words, she held him tight,
And when she would not part,
Felt his fists upon her
Until they broke her heart.

The battered girl awakened
In her home along the lane,
Her mother watching over,
Grieving, half insane.

"You've let this man walk over you
When you were out and wild,
And if you live you'll bear to him
This bastard's bastard child!"

"I know that what you say is true,"
Then swore as she felt cold,
"So I'll not let another do
To me as you have told."

Yet few took notice of her words
As she lay weak in bed,
For even with the doctor's care,
On the morrow she was dead.

Because of her condition,
The Church refused a plot,
So she was buried by the road
Among the paupers' lot

Where all that passed could see her shame
And all could make attacks
From those in fancy carriages
To those like Drunken Jack.

For when he saw it he did stand
Upon the tiny mound
Of earth that lay above her bones
Not yet sunken down.

He laughed believing he was free,
Another to pursue,
As visions flashed within his head
Of the many girls he knew.

For he'd not heard Priscilla's words
And, thus, he felt no dread
Dancing on her resting place
Above her final bed.

But when his foot again touched earth
The ground collapsed below,
The coffin splintered by his feet,
Entangled in her bones.

And as he fell, he saw her face
Just once – then all went black,
Impaled upon her wooden cross,
This man called Drunken Jack.

THE QUESTIONER'S APPRENTICE
Peter Adam Salomon

Galen woke with a start when the portly farmhand next to him stepped on his foot, digging the heel of a well-worn boot into his toes. Perhaps the farmhand just wanted him to pay attention in church, or maybe there was some other slight that Galen was only now being made to pay for. Either way, Galen didn't know and, really, didn't care.

He opened one brown eye, the color of bitter ale, and gave a half smile to the farmhand before turning back to where the Father read the liturgy. A ray of colored sunlight burned through the stained glass in the old stone walls and cast the Savior in dappled shadows.

Galen turned back to the farmhand and smiled that half smile again before yawning and closing his eyes. It took no more than a moment for that heel to be back on his toes.

"You fell asleep again, Galen," the Father said after Mass had ended. The small chapel was empty and the sunlight had shifted, leaving the Savior in darkness.

Galen smiled but remained silent as the Father sat down next to him on the hard wooden pew. Old bones creaked and the Father sighed.

"I always did wish we had better clothes for you, son," the Father said, resting a frail hand on Galen's shoulder and rubbing the frayed ends of the collar between his fingers. "So, how many jobs is this now?"

Galen stuck out his arm, the deep gold coloring so different from the paleness of the Father and, for that matter, most everyone else in the town. "One," he said, sticking up his thumb, "the blacksmith."

The Father laughed. "That was never going to work, you were always so afraid of fire. And then, of course, the blacksmith was injured in that terrible accident."

"Two, the baker." Galen's shoulders slumped down. "I could never figure out how to work the ovens properly."

"I know, that's why they sent you back here. The baker still burns my bread on purpose over that."

"And now three." Galen stuck another finger out. "The Questioner."

"You were always the curious one, ever since that soldier brought you here as an infant," the Father said. "Being the Questioner's apprentice seems the perfect place, even if it's not what I'd have chosen for you."

"Curiosity is good," a deep voice said from behind them.

Both Galen and the Father turned and the Questioner nodded to the Father before sitting next to them on the pew.

"But Questioning is about more than curiosity," the Questioner said with a shrug of his broad shoulders. Scabs ran around his arms, down to his fingers, small nicks and cuts barely healed. "You'll learn, Galen. If not, there are always stables to be cleaned."

"He's a fast learner," the Father said, patting Galen on the shoulder.

The Questioner and Galen watched the Father shuffle down the aisle, kicking up dust that sparkled in the colored sunlight, before leaving the chapel.

Outside, autumn had just begun to touch the trees, changing some but not all of the leaves. Children playing and screaming stopped moving and talking as the Questioner and Galen walked by, looking away or running to hide behind their parents.

The Questioner looked at Galen with a small shrug. "Parents have always used the threat of a visit from the Questioner as a way to keep unruly children in line," he said. "You'll get used to it eventually."

As they approached the opposite side of the square, where the servant's entrance to the castle was, the Questioner stopped in the middle of the road and turned around. He rested a meaty hand on Galen's back and forced him to turn as well.

"Look up at the sun," the Questioner said. "King and country expect us at the chapel Sunday for mass and confession. That, Galen, will be the next time you see daylight. Consider that lesson number one."

Through the gate in the outer wall, the Questioner led them into a small courtyard. The stable was a mass of activity, preparing for an after-Church outing. Sharp metallic sounds of hooves stomping on the blue cobbles filled the space. The Questioner bowed his head as the King and his family rode by. He slapped Galen on his neck to make him bow as well but Galen simply stared as the King smiled at his children on their smaller horses.

When they were alone again, the Questioner pushed Galen toward a small door set deep into an alcove of the inner wall. "You will have to learn to bow, boy, when the King passes by," he said as he pulled a key out of his pocket and opened the heavy wooden door.

"Yes, sir," Galen said, his voice swallowed by the dark passageway they had entered. Stairs went up, deeper into the interior of the wall, and the air chilled as they climbed.

Lost in the narrow chambers between the outer wall and the inner, the Questioner led Galen into a small series of rooms. There were no windows, just heavy wooden doors as thick as the walls that only moved with great effort. The smell of unwashed people and the copper tang of blood were overwhelming as they entered.

"Welcome to my home, Galen," the Questioner said, spreading his arms wide. "And yours, now, as well."

Along one stone wall a large wooden cabinet stood from floor to ceiling, the doors held closed with an elaborate lock. Heavy metal hooks studded the rock ceiling and walls, dripping chains. A bed was pushed up against another wall, with a small pile of blankets on the floor next to it. "That's yours," the Questioner said. "Won't be all that comfortable but it'll be warm at least."

Galen was about to answer when the door opened. A serving girl stepped inside, laden down with buckets. She stopped walking when she saw Galen but then turned to the Questioner with a small bow of her head, dark hair falling in front of her face, hiding her from view.

"Galen," the Questioner said, resting his hand heavily on his apprentice's shoulder. "This is Shanthi." The young woman bowed towards Galen and then hurried past them with her buckets. As she passed, the heavy stench of the cleaning liquid in her buckets was almost harsh enough to make him cough and his eyes began to water. Over her clothing, strips of cloth wound around her lithe figure and even though she'd yet to start cleaning they were already stained from prior use.

"She's still learning the routine around here," the Questioner said. "Lesson number two: the King had me remove her tongue since the last cleaning woman had a tendency to tell tales when she was drinking." The Questioner removed a different key from his pocket and unlocked another door for Shanthi. She rushed through and Galen caught a brief glimpse of cells and prisoners through the opening.

When they were alone, the Questioner walked up to the large cabinet. He pulled out yet another key and opened the lock. Inside, rows of odd mechanisms and instruments gleamed in the light of the flickering candles.

"The most important lesson of all," the Questioner said, "a master is nothing without his tools. The cook with his favorite pots, the blacksmith with his irons, and me, with these." He rested his hands upon a sharp blade, half hidden in shadows. "Each one is different, each has their own use. You could, of course, use any tool if you had to. After all, a hammer will cause tremendous pain even in untrained hands." The Questioner looked back at

GOTHIC BLUE BOOK

his apprentice, eyes sharp and piercing. "But Questioning is so much more than that, Galen. It is an art you are to learn and master. And each tool is a brush you will use to create that art."

He held up a small instrument, similar to the pliers Galen had grown familiar with during his brief stint as the blacksmith's apprentice but with far sharper tines. "This would pull out anything from tongues to toes but is designed specifically for fingernails. Though, really, I'd use this one," he pointed to the slightly larger pliers next to it, "for thumbs."

Next, the Questioner pointed to the even smaller pliers, briefly touching each in turn. "Toenails, eyelids, earlobes." Then the larger ones. "Teeth, tongue, nose, fingers."

Pointing to the knives, the Questioner continued. "Different blades, different depths of pain. You'll learn them all." He looked back at Galen. "But these are only tools. More important is what you ask, when, how. Each subject is different, with different levels of tolerance and, to be honest, different needs. It is the job of the Questioner to ask the right Questions, so that you can tell the King what he needs to know."

Galen looked over the tools hanging in their neat rows, metal glinting in the flickering light and smiled. "What's that?" he asked, pointing at a small wooden box on the floor of the cabinet.

The Questioner picked it up, fishing out yet another small key from his pocket with a laugh. Behind them the door opened and Shanthi started to sweep the room.

The Questioner lifted the lid of the small box to display a set of knives resting on black velvet within. They caught the flickering candlelight and seemed to glow in response. "These are pure silver, far too valuable to actually use." Again, the Questioner laughed, shaking his head with the sound. "It's a funny story, actually. One night a few years ago two bodies were found. It was a vicious crime, horrible. In the morning they found a man covered in blood. Since there had been a full moon the night before, the King was convinced the killer was a werewolf. Honestly, a werewolf! He commissioned these silver knives for me to use." The Questioner shrugged as both Galen and Shanthi listened to the story.

"Turned out he was just a drunk. Killed his friends over a gambling debt. I almost thought the King was disappointed. He's always going on about werewolves and vampires or morsus and whatnot. All those legends and myths." The Questioner locked the small box up and returned it to the floor of the cabinet.

"Morsus?" Galen asked, still looking at the small box with the silver knives.

"Well," the Questioner said, "as the old stories go, a vampire needs blood to survive and a werewolf needs flesh. They say the morsus requires pain to feed. Legends teach that vampires fear holy water, werewolves fear

80

silver and morsus fear fire." He smiled and then turned back to lock the cabinet. "Actually, 'morsus' is supposed to be the ancient's word for pain but no one speaks the language anymore, so who knows? Anyway, they're all myths, only the King actually believes any of it, so now I have this fancy set of useless knives."

The heavy wooden door to the room slammed open with a loud crash. The King and his guards rushed in, two of them dragging a young man. Blood trailed behind him, staining the freshly swept floor.

"This man," the King said to the Questioner, his voice thunderously loud in the small chamber, "tried to kill me." He drew his sword and waved it in the captive's face. "Who sent you? Why?"

The prisoner, hanging unconscious between the guards, didn't respond.

"Find out what he knows," the King said, pointing his sword at the Questioner. "I want to know who put him up to this!"

The guards dragged the prisoner to the center of the room where they attached chains to the shackles on his arms and lifted him into the air, hanging him from one of the metal hooks so that his toes barely touched the ground. The prisoner moaned, his head hanging down to his chest, but didn't wake up. When they were finished, the guards escorted the King from the room leaving the Questioner, his apprentice and Shanthi alone with the captive.

"Shanthi," the Questioner said, "that'll be all for today." He remained silent until she closed the door and then turned to Galen. "Watch and learn, apprentice."

The Questioner filled a bucket of water from a barrel in the corner and quickly tossed it over the prisoner. While the captive coughed, he went to the cabinet and took out one single knife. He held it up to the light and brushed it softly with a velvet cloth before checking it in the light again.

He smiled, his reflection caught in the blade. "This is my favorite," he said, speaking both to Galen and the prisoner without looking at either of them. He turned and walked up to the captive. "Did you know that you have three layers of skin?" the Questioner asked, his voice soft. "This blade is so fine it will peel off each layer individually. Do you know what that means?"

The captive tried to look away but the Questioner took a step to the side so that he remained in front of the prisoner.

"It means," the Questioner said, resting the tip of the blade on the prisoner's cheek, "that I can skin you three times."

By the time the King returned, the Questioner had learned that the prisoner had acted alone, to avenge the death of his family by the King's soldiers.

"Execute him," the King said, before leaving the Questioner and Galen alone with the captive again.

The Questioner, still with the prisoner's blood on his hands and face, turned to his apprentice. "Galen," he said, his voice even softer than before, "let's get this over with. I'm suddenly not feeling well." The Questioner took only one step towards the captive to carry out the sentence before he collapsed.

Galen rushed to his side and half carried the much larger man through another door to his private chambers. The Questioner fell into a shivering sleep almost as soon as his head hit the pillow.

Back in the main room, Galen sat on the edge of his own bed and watched the prisoner where he slowly swung back and forth from his chains. Galen stood and walked around the captive a number of times, watching the way the flickering candlelight reflected off the blood on the floor.

There was a soft knock and when Galen opened the door, Shanthi was there with more cleaning supplies. She pointed at the mess and Galen let her in, leaving her to the cleaning as he returned to the Questioner's side.

He watched his labored breathing for a while and was about to go back out to the main chamber when he heard the prisoner talking.

"Shhhh, Shanthi, it's all right," he said, the voice muffled by the partially open wooden door. Galen peeked around the corner and watched as Shanthi held an open vial to the prisoner's skin, collecting the blood slowly pouring out of him. "The poison I took causes far more pain than what that old man did to me." The words were almost hissed out, each syllable coming on its own labored breath.

Shanthi tried to say something but there were no words to be understood.

"You'll need more blood," he said and she pushed the vial deeper into his wounds, ignoring his cries. "It won't kill you, not unless it gets in your mouth or an opening in the skin."

She ran her fingers over his forehead, the only unblemished skin she could find, before carefully storing the vial of his blood in the cloths wound around her. She hid her tears from the prisoner but not from Galen where he spied on them, before leaving the room.

Galen counted as high as he knew how to count and then entered the chamber. The prisoner hung where he'd been left, his toes barely touching the ground. Once again, Galen walked a few circles around him, sniffing the air.

"You smell different than the other prisoners, back there," Galen said. "Is that the poison?"

The captive raised his head but he remained silent.

"It's causing you tremendous pain, isn't it?" Galen asked, taking a step closer to the prisoner, close enough to almost reach out and touch. "The poison, hurting you. It's killing the Questioner, isn't it?"

The prisoner looked away but Galen stepped closer still, until he was standing right in front of the man's bloody face.

"You smell—" Galen took a deep whiff of the air and smiled. "—delicious."

Galen lifted a hand up to the prisoner's face. His fingers stretched out in the flickering candlelight, the nails elongating like a cat's claws unsheathing. He rested his triple-jointed fingers in the captive's hair, one talon stabbing through skin and bone, deep into the pain centers of the brain. Two more claws pierced his torso as Galen fed.

The prisoner screamed but Galen inhaled the sound. He cried but Galen drank the tears like wine. He sobbed but his moans were nothing more than a symphony.

"Tell me," Galen said, his voice a hiss as he whispered to the prisoner, "why kill the King?"

The prisoner's eyes opened wide, the pupils gone. "Soldiers," he said, the word forced out through gritted teeth. "They came and killed our parents, took my newborn brother to execute by order of the King."

Galen stepped back, releasing the prisoner. The captive swung back and forth on his chains, his lungs heaving, trying to breathe. "When was this?"

The prisoner looked up, tears still pouring down his face, mixing with the blood from the hole in his skull. "A few months ago," he said, the words almost too soft to hear.

Galen sighed, the sound drawn out almost like a moan. "Why?"

"I don't know," the prisoner said. "No one knows."

Galen entered the Questioner's room, sitting down on the edge of the bed. The Questioner's eyelids fluttered open for a moment but then closed again.

"You smell like the prisoner," Galen said softly, leaning over the old man.

"What?" the Questioner asked, shivering in so much pain that the word could barely be heard through his shaking teeth.

"His blood infected you." Galen smiled and ran his fingers over the Questioner's face, the claws once more stretching out. "I'm sorry," he said, "there is no cure but me."

The next day, Galen sent word to the King that the Questioner had died, peacefully, in his sleep. As he waited for a response, he took the prisoner down from his chains and prepared both him and the Questioner for burial. Shanthi came in while he was finishing up.

"He's your brother, isn't he?" Galen asked, his voice soft.

She nodded and then backed in to a corner of the room as Galen walked over to her.

"I can't allow you to kill the King," he said, reaching out and taking the vial from the cleaning supplies she carried. "I'm sorry."

Galen pocketed it next to the ring of keys he'd taken from the Questioner, and turned away from Shanthi to face the King as he and his guards entered the room.

"I'll need a Questioner now, apprentice," the King said. "I guess that's to be you."

Galen bowed his head. "My Lord," he said, his voice whisper quiet, "thank you."

The King turned to go, but Galen kept talking, still staring at the floor.

"Your men scour the country," Galen said. "Killing certain infants. Why?"

The King stopped walking and turned back to face the new Questioner. "An old prophecy," he said. "That a morsus will end my reign. Just a myth everyone says, but my life and my kingdom are at stake, and I can never be too safe. Every so often a child is born, maybe their fingers are just a little too long, or have one joint too many…" The King stopped talking and shrugged.

The Questioner stood in the middle of the room, his feet firmly planted in the bloodstains left behind by the prisoner, and his just a little too long fingers curled into fists.

Behind him, Shanthi crawled to his side, wrapping herself around his legs. His long fingers wound through her hair, almost petting her.

"You killed my parents," the Questioner whispered.

The King's guards drew their swords but it was far too late.

The Questioner smiled.

"I am no myth."

REST
Jay Wilburn

He could see the water below and the pigs rooting on the hills beyond the cliffs. He could not tell if the men tending were feeding the herd or using them to dig out valuable fungus hidden in the ground to sell to wealthy tourists. Jacob understood details about life beyond the border of the cemetery, but felt no part in it any longer.

The stones closest to the pigs and water were short, white, and even marking the graves of soldiers. The sharply even pattern made the world spin in Jacob's vision when he tried to focus.

He lowered his eyes to the ground and looked back and forth between the civilian graves. A few of the plots sunk into the ground where old boxes underneath collapsed in hidden decay. Most created mounds of healthy grass. The fresher plots clumped with wads of dirt or stacked high with white, ceremonial stones.

"No one will pile them on my grave."

Jacob widened his eyes at the sound of his own voice. The light off the sea hurt. The words and the vibration did not feel real. Dead men were not supposed to speak.

The ancient stillness of the coastal cemetery in eastern Dullman barely south of Canada could have fooled people into thinking they had found a beautiful park. Jacob used to think of the town like another world where some families still stacked stones over graves and pigs herded on hillsides. This place was where his family died.

He turned away from the water.

Jacob open and closed his hands. He felt pain from blisters on his palms and dirt caked under his broken nails. He could not make them feel like a part of his body even with the intensity of the pain. He turned at his waist and felt the same about the organs hanging inside his body.

"I'm not alive."

A shape moved along the road in the distance beyond the graves. Jacob tried to spy it again between hills, but he allowed his eyelids to slide closed.

If we are dead, we need to find our spot in the Earth and rest.

Jacob felt cold inside and tried again to decide if the chorus of voices came from outside him in the invisible air or from inside his lifeless head. He still couldn't tell.

"I've been looking."

Jacob tasted blood in the back of his dry throat after he spoke. He tried to swallow the thick feeling behind his tongue, but he couldn't produce the saliva to do so.

The chorus sounded off again.

We need to look harder. If we are walking around, there is an empty plot waiting for us somewhere. Look again.

"Where exactly?"

We know where, don't we?

Jacob dropped his head and opened his eyes. He watched his feet move over pebbles pressed into the paths between rows of buried families. He walked closer to the gate in the sections of newer graves looking for his own family.

Jacob raised his eyes and scanned the wavy length of the iron fence in both directions. The erosion where the slope approached the street had pushed the sections of fence out in uneven curves. A living person walking along the road outside the gates would have great difficulty avoiding the tilting bars and the blocked sidewalk.

He was not on the outside, so he had no difficulty following the path.

The graves all looked the same after a while. Some stones had wider gaps in between. Some families divided their earth from their neighbors with low fences or concrete pillars.

Plots sat empty in spaces waiting for a body still working and playing in western Dullman to be planted one day. Other large tombstones marked the dirt over one body while the other side of the stone held a name and birth date, but waited for a few more numbers to be chiseled on the partner's side of the stone to complete the dash.

He thought there were the bones of a Supreme Court justice in Dullman Gardens, but Jacob had not found them.

Jacob saw a broad oak with fat branches stretching out laterally and close to the ground. Two bodies sat on one of the wider branches. He stopped and stared up at them.

The two boys spoke to one another in whispers.

Jacob whispered as he stood alone on the empty path. "Talking usually means they are alive."

After a moment, the boys slid off the branch and hung by their hands. They dropped onto the grass on their feet with the agility that is reserved for boys when they are young. They turned and ran for the edge of the grounds away from Jacob watching them.

"Yes, definitely alive."

Jacob watched the limb instead of the kids as they ran away. The thick branch appeared heavy. He knew it was crushingly heavy – deadly heavy. A utility truck that found itself passing under that branch could clip it with their equipment. They would probably ruin a ladder or bend a gear frame beyond repair, but they would cruise under before the limb snapped under its own weight. The sedan behind them would not be so lucky. A family in the next vehicle would meet that weight as it traveled through them to the Earth. They could have on seatbelts and infant car seats installed by helpful firefighters, but none of those things could beat the mass of the limb.

We know what you are thinking. We need to finish our journey down into the Earth.

Jacob shook himself and walked along the path under the massive limb.

"Show me where it is, if you are so insistent."

The chorus remained silent and he continued reading up and down the rows of stones. The whiteness of the stones glared in the sunlight and blurred the carved letters.

"I bet that bright whiteness is beautiful from a distance like the water and pig farmers on the hill. Everything is ugly up close."

We should know where this is by now and not be lost every time.

"Shut up."

He saw the spot and stopped. Jacob counted four stones with no spaces between them. He noticed that grass had begun to spring in a patchy pattern over the rough mounds. His family wasn't one that piled white stones. They were the kind that got crushed under falling limbs.

Jacob waited to cry, but tears were left to the living. He could not feel his heart or lungs any longer. His body just kept moving instead of resting like the girls.

He approached the graves looking for the space that must be his.

You need to let girls and me go. This is not what I want for you.

Jacob stopped short. This voice was not the chorus. It was a lone female voice and he felt certain he heard it outside himself.

He looked at the graves again and turned around scanning the hillside for motion. A man and woman in uniform walked up the path toward Jacob.

He cleared his throat and felt pain in his ears. "Did you say something?"

The radios clipped to their belts chirped in time with each other. Both officers turned down the volume before Jacob could make out the words. The doubling of the voices reminded him of the chorus.

The woman spoke, "Jacob Miller? I'm Officer Karen Dalton. Do you remember me? We went to the same church. I was friends with Elizabeth."

Jacob turned and looked back at the graves. If he ran, he could get there ahead of the officers. He still hadn't found his spot, so he probably didn't have time to dig. He wasn't afraid of being shot like living people feared, but if they grabbed him, they would drive him far away from where he was meant to rest.

Her voice was not the one he had heard a moment before he saw the police.

"Jacob?"

He turned to face the pair. They stood nearly in grabbing distance and they still walked forward.

"Yes, I remember you, Karen."

"What are you doing here?"

He lowered his eyes to stare at his feet. "I'm visiting my family."

The officers were quiet for long enough that Jacob looked up. He listened to their radios whispering.

Karen tilted her head. "Have you been here all day, Jacob?"

"Where else should I be?"

"Home, Jacob. Do you need us to take you to the hospital? You look sweaty and tired."

He glanced back at the graves.

If we go to their hospital, we will end up in their metal box in the basement. Do we prefer that to our spot in the Earth next to our loved ones?

Jacob turned his eyes back on the officers expecting to see them looking around for the invisible chorus. They stared at Jacob. The man pulled his radio off his belt and spoke into it with a series of numbers and words that did not mean anything to Jacob. He held it to his ear with his back to Jacob to listen to his own voices.

"I don't need a hospital."

Karen closed her warm fingers over Jacob's elbow. He hissed as if it burned. Jacob pulled back, but she held. His pull was weak and her grip did not have to squeeze too hard. He wondered how much pain he could still feel if he fought hard enough.

We should try it.

She said, "Don't be afraid, Jacob. You're just going to come with us. No big deal."

The male officer spun back and looked between his partner and Jacob. Jacob saw the man's free hand rise up level with his belt, but it didn't go to the butt of the gun.

Karen pulled and Jacob took a few steps forward to keep his balance. She pulled again and he walked beside her down the path to the gate. As they passed under the large branch, the red and blue lights from their car flashed off the trunk.

Jacob closed his eyes.

They don't understand what we are.

Jacob coughed and swallowed. "Karen, you know the city has a law that you can't cut the limbs on these oaks no matter how big they get. They just tie metal cables around them to keep them from falling, but you can't beat gravity. Everything goes into the Earth where it belongs."

She put a hand on his shoulder and he hissed again.

"I'm sorry, Jacob. It's not your fault."

She pushed down on his head and he opened his eyes toward the ground. The patrol car sat sideways blocking the entrance to the cemetery. Jacob slid into the back of the car where she directed him and she closed the door. His knees jammed into plastic wall between his seat and the front.

Jacob stared at his legs as they drove away from his family and the sea.

Karen opened the door and guided him out onto the sidewalk in front of the townhouse where he used to live with his girls. Jacob could see the yellow slip of paper attached the front, glass door of the house.

The male officer stayed in the car writing as Karen stood beside Jacob.

"Are you still in the house, Jacob? Did the foreclosure go through?"

"They haven't kicked me out yet."

He started up the front walk and pulled open the glass door. His hand rested on the knob with the security lock over the top. He moved his body to hide it from view. After he heard the engine, he turned to see the cruiser turn under the splintered tree missing its limb at the end of the street.

Jacob let the glass door bang closed and he walked back east in the opposite direction of the officers and the place his girls were crushed.

He stared at his feet as he limped through the last few miles back to the Gardens. People spoke to him from porches and the other side of the road. They blended with his own chorus of voices.

We do not have to obey the authority of the living.

"Did you want me to fight her?" Jacob asked the ground.

We have a destination and we are stalling.

"I'm walking as fast as I can. Not bad for a dead man either."

We are moving slower than the other dead. They made it into ground much faster than us.

"I'm doing the best I can."

Jacob stepped out into the road to avoid the leaning spikes at the top of the iron fence. A car swerved wide around him and laid down on their horn. The headlight swept over and off him as they passed in the growing darkness.

Jacob walked through the gate and back under the large limb.

He looked up when he reached the stones. He could not recall what order they were in and he could not read them in the dark. He felt over their surface making out Christy, Holly, and Tamatha. He traced every letter of Elizabeth Miller, mother and wife. Jacob bowed his head and found the ability to cry.

We do not cry.

Jacob didn't answer, but felt around the grass and loose dirt as he sobbed. He knew he had left what he needed here before a previous interruption. He hit his head on the edge of his wife's stone, but did not react.

Jacob found the handle and stood slowly.

We need to finish this.

Jacob stared at the black ground. "I don't have a space here. I don't know where to start."

We will make a space. Do we want to stay on top of the Earth wandering to and fro forever?

Jacob stabbed the blade into the Earth over his wife's grave. He pressed down with his foot to drive the shovel as far as it could go.

"I'm sorry, Beth. We'll be together again soon."

This is not what I want.

Jacob paused at the sound of the single voice. He looked over the faint whiteness of her marker.

"Are you talking to me?"

You need to go to the hospital. You are sick.

The chorus argued. *We are dead.*

Jacob nodded. "We are dead."

I am dead, Jacob. You are alive and I want you to stay that way. I don't know what it is called, but you aren't thinking clearly. You think you are dead, but you are not.

He leaned down on the handle and lifted out a shovel full of dirt. Jacob tossed it aside and drove the blade back in next to the hole he had started.

"I just want to rest, Beth. I want the family together again. You shouldn't be in the ground alone."

I don't want this.

"You don't want us to be together?"

I am not in the ground and neither are the girls, Jacob, and you are not dead.

He dumped another shovel full and drove into the hole again.

He laughed and wiped sweat from his lips onto his sleeve.

"We paid a lot to have four funerals. We marked your spots so we wouldn't lose them."

We lose them all the time.

Jacob gritted his teeth at the chorus.

Jacob, I came back to save you from this. If I had survived, you would not want this for me.

Jacob leaned on the handle and cried.

The chorus spoke up. *We need to finish this.*

"We need to finish this, Beth."

Digging a hole because you think you are dead doesn't finish anything. The girls and I are beyond all this. You can't reach me with a shovel. Go to the hospital. Let me save you. I love you, Jacob. Do what I ask in this because you love me. What happened to me and the girls wasn't your fault.

"Beth, please, just let me rest."

The beam of the flashlight rested on his back washing out the dark world.

"Jacob, step away from that shovel."

He lifted his head and glanced around the inside of the blinding beam of light.

"Beth, is that you?"

"It's me, Jacob. I'm Officer Karen Dalton. I picked you up earlier. Beth is dead and you are acting crazy. You should have stayed at your house. Now you are trespassing. We need to take you in. I'll need your hands away from the shovel."

Jacob stepped back and lifted his hands.

We need to finish this. They can't hurt us when we are already dead. Run. Let them shoot.

Jacob swallowed. "She says I'm sick and I need to go to the hospital."

"Who, Jacob?"

"Beth. She says I'm sick and if I love her I'll go to the hospital even though I am dead."

"Why are you back here, Jacob?"

Jacob bowed his head and closed his eyes. "Looking for my grave."

Karen pulled Jacob's hands behind his back and closed the cuffs over his wrists.

"We'll take you to the hospital like Beth told you."

Jacob walked between the officers as the flashlight showed the broad limb and cast a deep shadow across the path.

He looked into the shadow. "I'm dead. They can't help me. I'm only doing this to make her happy."

Karen patted Jacob's shoulder. "I think they can fix the kind of dead you are feeling. Beth is right. We'll listen to her this time."

ABOUT THE CONTRIBUTORS

MEG BELVISO lives in New York City where she is a staff editor at *Angels on Earth*, a bi-monthly magazine about real-life encounters with angels. As a freelancer she's written for many different properties, from Looney Tunes to Dexter's Laboratory, and children's biographies from Steve Jobs to Alfred Hitchcock. This year she's had stories included in *Fight Like a Girl*, a fantasy collection spotlighting female heroines, and *Puzzle Box*, an anthology whose tales share a secret origin.

DIE BOOTH lives in Chester, England in a tiny house with four fireplaces and enjoys playing violin, drinking tea and exploring dark places. Die's work has been featured in three Cheshire Prize for Literature anthologies and has recently appeared in *The Fiction Desk*, *Litro*, *For All Eternity* from Dark Opus Press and Prime's *Bloody Fabulous* anthology amongst others. You can also read several of Die's stories in the 2011 anthology *Re-Vamp* co-edited by L.C. Hu. Forthcoming work is due to appear in *The Art of Fairytales* edited by Sarah Grant and Die's first novel *Spirit Houses* will be available in 2013. You can visit Die at http://diebooth.wordpress.com/.

MELISSA J. DAVIES is a writer originally from London now living in Perth, Australia. Melissa has always been intrigued by ghost stories, bloody history and characters that are more than a little untrustworthy. Melissa has published several short stories and poems of various genres but likes gothic fiction the best. She is currently working on her first novel.

LANCE DAVIS is a husband, father of two, and a lifelong fan of the horror genre. He has written numerous short stories and is currently working on his first novel. He is a manager for a company where he lives, but his goal is to one day separate himself from it and immerse himself fully into his writing.

NICOLE DEGENNARO currently works as a copy editor for a science publisher and lives in the Hudson Valley area of New York. Although she studied journalism at Purchase College, her heart has always belonged to fiction writing. Her short story *Home Coming* will appear in the upcoming anthology *Scarea Spitless* from Silly Tree Anthologies, due out in October. You can learn more about Nicole at her blog: http://nicoledegennaro.wordpress.com/.

MATHIAS JANSSON is a Swedish art critic and poet. He has been published in magazines as *The Horror Zine Magazine*, *Dark Eclipse*, *Schlock*, *The Sirens Call* and *The Poetry Box*. He has also contributed to several anthologies from Horrified Press and James Ward Kirk Fiction as *Suffer Eternal anthology Volume 1-3*, *Hell Whore Anthology Volume 1-3*, *Barnyard Horror and Serial Killers Tres Tria*. For more about Jansson visit http://mathiasjansson72.blogspot.se/

K. TRAP JONES is a writer of horror novels and short stories. With a sadistic inspiration from Dante Alighieri and Edgar Allan Poe, his temptation towards narrative folklore, classic literary works and obscure segments within society lead to his demented writing style of "filling in the gaps" and walking the jagged line between reality and fiction. His novel THE SINNER (Blood Bound Books, 2012) won the Royal Palm Literary Award. He is also a member of the Horror Writer's Association and can be found lurking around Tampa, Florida.

MICHAEL KELLAR is a writer, poet, and occasional online bookseller living in Myrtle Beach, SC. His most recent print publication was a horror story appearing in the anthology *Side Show 2: Tales of the Big Top and the Bizarre*, and he has recently had stories accepted for two upcoming anthologies, *Metastasis* and *The Ghoul Saloon*.

EDWARD J. MCFADDEN III, is an editor and author of more than ten published books of fiction and over 50 short stories. His most recent works include his novels *The Black Death of Babylon* (Post Mortem Press) and *Our Dying Land* (Padwolf Publishing, Inc.) His novelette *Starwisps* was selected for the 2012 Tangent Recommended Reading list. He lives on Long Island, NY, with his wife Dawn, their daughter Samantha, and a mutt named Oli. See www.edwardmcfadden.com for all things Ed.

JESSICA MCHUGH is an author of speculative fiction that spans the genre from horror and alternate history to epic fantasy. A member of the Horror Writers Association and a 2013 Pulp Ark nominee, she has devoted herself to novels, short stories, poetry, and playwriting. Jessica has had thirteen books published in five years, including the bestselling *Rabbits in the Garden*, *The Sky: The World* and the gritty coming-of-age thriller, *PINS*. More info on her speculations and publications can be found at JessicaMcHughBooks.com.

GEORGINA MORALES from early on felt fascinated by the horror genre. The stunning covers tantalized her with promises of endless darkness and obscure tales. While other girls dreamed of becoming princesses, her young mind weaved stories of madness to fit those covers. Years later, after settling in New England, she felt perfectly at home surrounded by dark woods and abandoned buildings. It is from those places and memories that she writes, spinning stories from inside the obscure corridors of the mind where not many venture and very few come out alive. Stalk her on Facebook: www.facebook.com/pages/Perpetual-Night-by-Georgina-Morales/159894374059399

CORTNEY PHILIP writes fucked up fairy tales for grown-up kids. Her work has appeared in *The First Line, elimae, Feathertale Review, At-Large Magazine, Gothic Blue Book: Revenge Edition*, and all around town. She regrets almost everything.

JENNIFER A. SMITH writes tales of horror and unease while Stella, the tabby cat, keeps watch. Jennifer was born in Minnesota during the second half of the twentieth century. Coffee and diet cola fuel her fanciful thoughts; working at a small town post office provides a fearful insight into the darkness of men's souls. A previous story, *Last Summer*, was published in the Gothic Blue Book – Revenge edition.

K.R. SMITH is a full-time Information Technology Specialist and a part-time writer, frustrated by his inability to get any meaningful programming code to rhyme and still function properly. While mainly interested in writing short stories of the horror genre, he occasionally delves into poetry, songwriting, and the visual arts. Further escapades are available on his blog at www.theworldofkrsmith.com or on Twitter as @WOKRSmith.

PETER ADAM SALOMON graduated Emory University in Atlanta, GA with a BA in Theater and Film Studies in 1989. He has served on the Executive Committee of the Boston and New Orleans chapters of Mensa as the Editor of their monthly newsletters and was also a Judge for the 2006 Savannah Children's Book Festival Young Writer's Contest. He is a member of the Society of Children's Book Writers and Illustrators, the Horror Writers Association, the International Thriller Writers and The Authors Guild and is represented by the Erin Murphy Literary Agency. His debut novel, HENRY FRANKS, was published by Flux in September 2012. His next novel, ALL THOSE BROKEN ANGELS, a ghost story set in Savannah, GA, will be released by Flux in Fall 2014. Peter Adam Salomon lives in St. Petersburg, FL with his wife Anna and their three sons: André Logan, Joshua Kyle and Adin Jeremy.

JAY WILBURN lives in coastal swamps of South Carolina with his family. He has published a number of horror and speculative fiction stories including his novels *Loose Ends* and *Time Eaters*. He has a piece in *Best Horror of the Year Volume Five* with editor Ellen Datlow. He is a proud member of the Horror Writers Association and is a featured author in the Dark and Bookish tour and documentary. Follow his many dark thoughts at JayWilburn.com and @AmongTheZombies on Twitter.

Made in the USA
Charleston, SC
07 November 2013